OPENING BID

"Think about my offer?" Alicia Baxter asked.

"I decided talk was cheap," Fargo said.

"Would you make up your mind if you had more than talk?" Alicia asked.

"It'd sure help," Fargo said blandly.

He stayed unmoving as her lips came down on his, soft at first, then growing strong, pressing, moving to open wider. She pulled back and he watched her hand move to the buttons of her white shirt. She undid them, slowly, until the blouse hung open, giving him a tantalizing look at her breasts. Then she made a quick, wiggling motion with her shoulders, and her shirt came off. Wordlessly she stretched her legs out, unbuttoned her jeans and drew them off.

As she came naked into his arms, Fargo thought that her sister Aggie would have to go a long way to top this bid for his services. Of course, he was more than willing to let Aggie try. . . .

THE TRAILSMAN 65

RIVER KILL

by

Jon Sharpe

A SIGNET BOOK

NEW AMERICAN LIBRARY

NAL BOOKS ARE AVAILABLE AT QUANTITY DISCOUNTS
WHEN USED TO PROMOTE PRODUCTS OR SERVICES.
FOR INFORMATION PLEASE WRITE TO PREMIUM MARKETING DIVISION,
NEW AMERICAN LIBRARY, 1633 BROADWAY,
NEW YORK, NEW YORK 10019

The first chapter of this book previously appeared in *Fargo's Woman*, the sixty-fourth volume in this series.

SIGNET TRADEMARK REG. U.S. PAT. OFF. AND FOREIGN COUNTRIES
REGISTERED TRADEMARK—MARCA REGISTRADA
HECHO EN CHICAGO. U.S.A.

SIGNET, SIGNET CLASSIC, MENTOR, ONYX, PLUME,
MERIDIAN and NAL BOOKS are published by NAL PENGUIN INC.,
1633 Broadway, New York, New York 10019

First Printing, May, 1987

1 2 3 4 5 6 7 8 9

PRINTED IN THE UNITED STATES OF AMERICA

The Trailsman

Beginnings . . . they bend the tree and they mark the man. Skye Fargo was born when he was eighteen. Terror was his midwife, vengeance his first cry. Killing spawned Skye Fargo, ruthless, cold-blooded murder. Out of the acrid smoke of gunpowder still hanging in the air, he rose, cried out a promise never forgotten.

The Trailsman, they began to call him, all across the West: searcher, scout, hunter, the man who could see where others only looked, his skills for hire but not his soul, the man who lived each day to the fullest, yet trailed each tomorrow. Skye Fargo, the Trailsman, the seeker who could take the wildness of a land and the wanting of a woman and make them his own.

*1861, a place called Wildcat Den—
where the mighty Mississippi is a
flowing border between Iowa and Illinois . . .*

1

Something was wrong.

He sensed it, felt it, knew it.

Instinct. Sixth sense. Premonition. There were many names for it and he believed in it. He'd seen its force too many times before. Every wild creature knew it, lived by it . . . or died by it. Something was wrong, the big man with the lake-blue eyes grunted again inwardly.

His hands grew tight on the reins of the horse and he felt the hairs at the back of his neck stiffen. Skye Fargo rode the magnificent Ovaro, with its jet-black fore and hind quarters and pure white midsection, along the edge of the river, and his eyes flicked to the green wall of dense foliage at his left that grew almost to the water's edge. He'd followed along the riverbank for the last few miles and now he found himself unsure whether he'd been wise in doing so. The sound of the Mississippi as it lapped its shores and the shouts of keelmen on passing flatboats made just enough noise to interfere with his wild-creature hearing. The green wall of foliage remained impenetrable to his ears as well as his eyes, and he was glad when he finally came into sight of the bend in the river a few hundred yards ahead.

It marked the meeting place and the early afternoon sun marked the hour. He was pretty damn near exactly on time, Fargo grunted as he frowned. The letter had said a boat would be there at the shore of the bend where a black willow grew out over the river's edge. He could see the big willow but no boat, and he was still frowning into the distance when he caught the sudden movement in the dense foliage at his left. The big Colt seemed to fly from the holster at his side into his hand as the riders burst from the trees. Five of them, he saw, guns in hand, and he got off two shots as he dived from the saddle. He saw two of the men go down as he hit the soft mud of the riverbank and rolled into the water.

A half-dozen bullets skittered along the water as he went under the surface, all fired too fast and too wildly. He stayed underwater, swam downriver, and surfaced a dozen yards away. He saw one horseman racing toward him along the riverbank while another had galloped upriver. The Colt in his hand, Fargo brought the gun out of the water and fired just as the horseman spied him. The man toppled from his horse and hadn't hit the ground when Fargo's long legs splashed through the water and onto the shore. Water spraying from his racing figure, he ran for the trees as the other two whirled when they heard his shot. They saw his dripping form disappear into the trees, he knew, and he dived into thick brush and heard the two riders pull to a halt, their feet hit the ground as they leapt from their mounts.

He crouched low, still as a chameleon on a leaf, and forced himself to ignore the trickle of water that ran down his nose. Unable to see clearly out of the thick brush, he heard the two figures fan out on both sides of him and begin to move through the trees. He listened, heard the one on his left come closer, and he waited another thirty seconds longer. The man had come within six feet of him when Fargo snapped to his feet, his finger on the trigger, the Colt raised and all but aimed. The man heard him, spun to fire, but Fargo's shot exploded first and the man's chest collapsed as he all but catapulted backward and slammed into a tree trunk.

Fargo dropped down the instant the bullet left the gun, and heard the shot whistle over his head. He waited, but there was no other shot. Instead, he heard the sound of the figure running through the underbrush, and he rose and spotted the man as he raced from the trees and vaulted onto his horse. Fargo lowered the Colt as the rider galloped out of sight along the riverbank, and his lips were a tight, thin line as he pushed his way past low-hanging willow branches to where he'd left the Ovaro. He paused to examine the lifeless forms that lay scattered along the way. Hired gunhands, he guessed, scruffy outfits, cracked leather boots with rundown heels, frayed shirts, and only the usual possessions on them of chewing tobacco, cigars, extra kerchiefs, and a few silver dollars. Fargo's mouth remained tight as he swung onto the Ovaro, still soaking wet and a lot less than happy.

The attackers had been after him. There was no mistake about that. They'd been lying in wait and had come out charging. But, as with most hired gunhands, there had been more charging than shooting, and they had paid the price for it. All but one, who was probably still hightailing it, Fargo grunted. The river bend was still a few hundred yards away and he rode slowly and felt grateful for the hot sun that immediately began to dry his clothes even as he rode. He reached the big black willow where it leaned out over the water, stopped in the sun just short of it, and dismounted. There was no boat in sight and he peeled off wet clothes down to his underwear bottoms, strapped his gun belt back on, and sat down after he'd hung his things in the sun.

The Mississippi flowed lazily south, fairly wide where the bend curved, but it narrowed below and above. The red man had named it Mississippi, the Father of Waters, and three hundred years back the Spaniard

De Soto had crossed its ever-changing surface. Fargo let his thoughts idle and he remembered how the settlers along the upper reaches of the river where it flowed into the Minnesota territory called it a willful woman, sometimes quiet and peaceful, sometimes raging and overflowing, wide in some places, narrow in others, and always unfathomable and unpredictable. He let thoughts break off as he saw two boats come around the bend, and he recognized them at once. Arks, the rivermen called them, the term as cynical as accurate. On a base of flatboats and old scows, the arks were built to carry entire families, some fashioned into floating houses with small stone chimneys. They were given their name of arks because they often carried livestock as well as people, the larger ones often resembling a floating farmyard with horses, cows, a stable at one end, and hens, rabbits, and extra cartwheels on the roof.

They came in all sizes and shapes, and the two he watched go by were very different from each other. The first had a flat-roofed structure built to the very edges of both sides, with only enough room fore and aft for a keelman and two polemen to work. The other was twice the size, a long, low scow with a cabin built in the center of it and a half-dozen goats, horses, and children aft of the house. Some arks had sails but more were worked by oars and polemen moving with the currents. Fargo watched the two boats slowly move upstream, to finally sail out of sight. He settled back and watched at least six more of the arks move past him as the time dragged on. One particularly large ark carried a Conestoga wagon on it, he noted. For those who chose it, the Mississippi seemed a watery avenue into the northern territories, its perils less than those of the grueling dangers of wagon trains.

Many lived to realize their mistake. And many died knowing it. The mighty Mississippi held its own perils, from floods and storms to river pirates and the Indians who waited where the river ran shallow. There were many such places, and many arks that never sailed any farther up the great river. But others still sailed, all their possessions aboard their floating homes, able to take more than they could on a wagon train, ignoring the truth that while they floated, they were not really mobile. He wondered if any more of them reached their goals than those who traveled by land. He closed away idle musings and saw that the sun had dried his clothes; he frowned as he peered across the river. He'd waited over an hour, closer to two, and no one had come, and the sun was curving down toward the horizon. He dressed, dug into his shirt pocket, and pulled out the small square of notepaper. It was still slightly soggy, and he unfolded it carefully and stared down at the now-smudged ink.

The letter had reached him general delivery after he'd finished breaking trail for Bill Alderson's long range drive in Missouri. He'd no commitments waiting, and the money that had come with the letter was more than a surprise. It was the kind of money a man had to have a damn good reason to turn down, and he remembered frowning as he'd counted the five hundred dollars in U.S. currency. He squatted down along the riverbank now as he read the letter again:

Dear Mr. Fargo:

The money enclosed speaks for itself. I know the best never comes cheap and you're the best, the Trailsman. Harry Tallbutt told me how you saved his herd in South Dakota a few years back.

I'll meet you, first Monday of next month, one hour past noon, at the bend in the Mississippi just above Wildcat Den. If you can't come, I'll expect this money returned.

A. Baxter
for the Baxter Ranch

P.S. I'll be coming by boat.

Fargo folded the letter and returned it to his pocket as he swept the river again with a quick glance. A cargo flatboat moved slowly near the opposite bank, and the rest of the boats that rounded the bend floated slowly on their way. None came toward him, though he and the Ovaro were in full view on the bank. Fargo felt the frown dig into his forehead. Someone had tried to kill him and now he'd been left waiting like a bride at the church. He wanted some answers. He spun and climbed onto the Ovaro, sent the horse away from the riverbank at a canter, pushed through the willows, and found a road on the other side. The day was still clinging as he took the road south toward Wildcat Den. He didn't plan on going into the town unless it was necessary. The way the letter to him had been signed made it seem as though the Baxter Ranch was a well-known outfit.

He slowed as he saw the market wagon with the closed sides and the low side panels, a lone driver holding the reins of a heavy-bodied brown mare. The man reined up as Fargo came alongside, curiosity lining an oval face. "Looking for the Baxter Ranch," Fargo said. "You know where I might find it?"

"Take the fork by the big rock, stay on it till you reach two twisted aspen. Turn right and keep riding along the road till you come to it. 'Bout another half-hour's ride," the man said.

"Much obliged," Fargo returned, and sent the Ovaro on until he found the big rock and turned right. He came to the twisted aspens in time and rode on in a fast canter until he saw the ranch, a large spread with an impressive, stone ranch house. Night had just begun to settle down when he rode up to the big house and paused to scan the corrals that fanned out behind it, each one fenced into small units filled with sheep, mostly cheviots and Suffolk, he noted.

Two ranch hands paused to watch him as he dismounted, one as tall as a small tree, at least six foot, six inches, he guessed, with a long, narrow face to match his body. The other one seemed short next to him, a medium-built man with a crooked nose. The two men watched as he went to the ranch-house door and knocked. The door was opened after a moment and he found himself staring at a young woman in a floor-length house dress of dark blue with red bows down the front of it. Black hair framed a more than normally attractive face of high cheekbones, pale-white skin that gave her a delicacy, thin black eyebrows that arched over very dark-brown eyes, and full red lips. She was fairly tall, and a small waist made her breasts seem larger than they probably were, and the dark eyes regarded him with interest as they took in the intense, chiseled handsomeness of his face.

"Came to see Mr. Baxter," Fargo said, and saw her eyes narrow a fraction as she peered at him for a long moment.

"There is no Mr. Baxter, not since he died a little over a year ago," she said.

The frown furrowed Fargo's brow at once. "How come he sent me a letter last month?" Fargo asked, and saw the smooth, pale-white brow take on a small furrow of its own.

"I don't understand?" she said.

"That makes two of us," Fargo grunted. "And the letter."

"That's impossible. My father couldn't have sent you a letter last month," she said.

"Your father?" Fargo echoed in surprise.

"That's right," the young woman snapped. "And if someone sent you a letter, they're playing some kind of sick joke on you."

"Pretty damn expensive joke," Fargo said calmly, and decided to stay silent about the ambush.

Her nicely molded chin lifted and the dark-brown eyes surveyed him with skepticism. "I'd like to see this letter," she said.

He started to reach into his pocket when a voice called from inside the house. "What is it, Alicia?" it asked.

"Alicia?" Fargo echoed, and his brow lifted.

"That's right, Alicia Baxter," she said coolly, and Fargo heard the steps as the door was pulled open wider.

Fargo took in the man, well-built, broad-shoulders, clothed in a black shirt, and with a gun belt hung at the right length for his arms. He saw a face many women undoubtedly called handsome, but he took in the cruel line of the man's mouth and the coldness of his gray eyes.

"This man claims Father sent him a letter last month," Alicia Baxter explained, her eyes still on Fargo.

"Correction," Fargo cut in. "Somebody sent me a letter. I didn't say who."

"Who are you, mister?" the man barked authoritatively.

"Name's Fargo . . . Skye Fargo," the Trailsman answered. "Who're you, seeing as how we're all getting to know each other?"

"This is Fred Ronan," the young woman answered. "He's my ranch manager." She speared Fargo with a cool glance again. "That letter, please," she said, and made the request sound like an order.

Fargo took the letter from his pocket, handed it to her, and watched the frown deepen across her brow as she read it. "It's signed A. Baxter, as you can see. I'm wondering what the *A* stands for, now," Fargo remarked casually as she finished reading.

Her dark eyes snapped as she looked up at him from the letter. "It certainly doesn't stand for Alicia, if that's what you're thinking," she said. "I didn't send it and I know nothing about it."

"Somebody sent it," Fargo said.

"You heard the lady. She doesn't know anything about it," Ronan cut in protectively.

"Yes, I heard her." Fargo smiled affably and saw the man's face darken.

"You saying she's lying?" Ronan growled.

"Some people have short memories," Fargo said.

Ronan stepped out of the house threateningly. "I ought to break your face for that, mister," he said. "You watch your damn tongue or I'll teach you a lesson."

"Fred, stop," Alicia Baxter cut in, and put her hand on the man's arm. "Don't start anything with him."

"I'd listen to the little lady." Fargo smiled again.

Ronan kept up his threatening glower, but Fargo saw him take in the power of the big man in front of him and, more than that, the quiet, calm confidence that held its own message.

"You get off this ranch, mister. Alicia doesn't know anything about your damn letter," Ronan said, and let Alicia pull him back.

"Maybe not. But somebody does. I aim to find out," Fargo said almost pleasantly. He let his glance hold on the young woman for a moment longer. Her dark eyes met his with bold strength.

"If you do, let me know. I'd be interested," she said.

Fargo let his smile broaden. She was cool, very much in charge of herself. "I'll do that." He nodded as he turned away and swung onto the Ovaro. The treelike figure and the other man were still in place, looking on, Fargo saw as he slowly rode away. He put the pinto into a trot and let the night swallow him up in its dark blanket.

When he was far enough from the ranch, he turned, sent the horse up a low hill, and doubled back. A line of hawthorns let him come close to the house, and he moved to the very edge of the trees, swung to the ground, and rested on one knee. He watched as the lights went out in the bunkhouse to one side and focused his gaze on the ranch house. Maybe Alicia

Baxter knew nothing about the letter. Her frown had seemed real as she'd read it. But he'd seen frowns that seemed real before. It seemed a lot of coincidence that it was signed with her initial. There was one thing more he'd noted: she hadn't asked him in to talk about the letter signed with her name and her initial. Normal curiosity would've dictated that. Instead, she'd been interested only in dismissing it and him. Too interested and too peremptory.

If she knew about the letter, he mused, did she know about the attempt to kill him? His thoughts broke off as he saw the front door of the ranch house open and Ronan leave. He watched the man go into the bunkhouse by a side door and returned his eyes to the ranch house. The living-room light stayed on for almost an hour longer until it finally went out.

Fargo waited, watched as a lamp was turned on in a room on the second floor of the big house. He caught a glimpse of the young woman as she passed the window and saw the flash of bare shoulders before the lamp was turned off. Draping the Ovaro's reins across a low branch, he left the trees in a low, loping crouch, crossed the open space in front of the house, and spied a side door. His hand closed around the knob and found it turned at once, and the door swung open to let him slip into the darkness of the house.

On steps soft as a bobcat's tread, he crept through the hallway, found the short staircase, and climbed to the second floor. The first room was empty, the door hanging open, but the next one offered a closed door. Once again, his big hand swallowed the doorknob, and he turned slowly, eased the door open, and stepped into the bedroom, a big, queen-size bed near the window, the slender form in the very center of it. He crept forward, dropped to one knee as Alicia Baxter turned over and he glimpsed a long, bare arm, the thin strap of a silk nightgown over the shoulder. He rose, took three long-legged strides to reach the bed. The young woman's eyes snapped open just as he brought one hand down over her mouth. He saw the surprise in her dark eyes as she stared up at him. Only surprise, no fear, he noted with a flash of admiration.

"Time to talk some more, honey," he said.

and your Italian palate," it said. "Perks enjoyed themselves, but I think you know who did," Fargo said.

"Why would I care?" snapped

2

She made a muffled sound under his hand and he pressed down harder. "No noise," he growled, and felt her lips move as she tried to sink her teeth into the side of his palm. "Dammit," Fargo swore, pressed harder, and saw her wince. "I just want to talk," he said. "You can do it the easy way or the hard way." He waited, saw her dark eyes glare up at him from above his hand. "I'll take my hand away if you give me your word not to yell," he said.

Her glare stayed as she considered the offer, and she finally nodded. "Your word?" he said, and she nodded again. He slowly lifted his hand from her face and stepped back as she swung from the bed, the silk nightgown revealing slightly long but nicely curved twin cream-white mounds. She yanked the nightgown up as she reached for a shawl and flung it around her shoulders.

"Don't hide it," he remarked. "You've a right nice shape there, Alicia."

Her eyes flashed dark fire at him. "You didn't come sneaking in here to give me compliments," she snapped.

"That's true, but I always stop to admire a good-looking horse and a good-looking woman," Fargo said.

"I'm flattered. Now get out of here," Alicia hissed.

"Not so fast. I want some answers, honey," Fargo said.

"I gave you all the answers I have," she said angrily.

"Somehow, I just don't think that's so." Fargo smiled. Let's start with the letter."

"I told you, I didn't send it," Alicia Baxter snapped.

"Maybe not, but I think you know who did," Fargo said.

"Why would I know that?"

"You tell me."

"I've nothing to tell you. Why do you think I do?" Alicia insisted.

"Your name, your initial, your ranch," Fargo said. "And you don't know anything at all? Bullshit, sweetie." He paused, took in the tall slenderness of her body as the silk nightgown clung to it. "You're going to be chilly in that outfit," he said, and she frowned back. "I think I'll have to take you with me until your memory improves."

"My memory won't improve, and you stay away from me," she said. She took a step backward and her eyes narrowed at him. "Maybe there is something," she said.

"Now, that's better." Fargo nodded and watched her turn to a night table with a porcelain jewelry box on it. She reached for the box, closed her hand around it, and suddenly she was an explosion of movement as her arm came up and she flung the box through the window. It smashed the glass and the crash sounded like a clap of thunder in the stillness. "You little bitch," Fargo said as he grasped her arm. "You gave me your word."

"I promised not to yell," she snapped as he heard the shouts and footsteps from outside. He spun her around and flung her half across the big bed. She bounced on her stomach, and long, lovely legs kicked upward. But he hadn't time to stay and admire them as he ran for the door.

"Miss Baxter, you all right?" he heard a voice call out from under the window as he bolted down the stairs and raced out the side door. He ran toward the rear of the house and glimpsed more figures coming from the bunkhouse. Staying in a low, crouching lope, he headed for the trees and the Ovaro.

"Alicia, what is it?" he heard Ronan call.

"Over there," Alicia shouted back from the window, and Fargo cursed silently. He was at the trees when the shots split the night and he heard the bullets slam into bark at his left. He leapt onto the pinto and sent the horse swerving in and out of the trees until he'd cleared the woods and crossed a gentle slope under a half-moon. He slowed when a large sugar maple beckoned to him at the top of the long slope. He halted under its wide, low branches, which formed a circle of blackness and offered good shelter for the night. He unsaddled the horse, took down his bedroll, and undressed down to the bottoms of his underwear. He placed the big Colt in its holster alongside his hand as he lay down and stretched out. The thoughts that paraded through his head were a disturbing procession.

Alicia Baxter was lying about something, he was convinced. Had someone sent the letter to him in her name? He wondered. If so, why? He grimaced, the question a dead end at the moment. Or had Alicia Baxter really sent it and had a change of heart? Another large why presented itself at once. Maybe someone was making her have a change of heart, Fargo frowned. But the parade of questions only brought others when he needed answers, not more questions. He had the letter and little else, and his lips drew tight as he thought about the gunhands who had ambushed him. Had they done the same to whoever had waited to meet him, only with more success?

He frowned into the night as he thought about picking up and leaving. He had filled his part of the deal. He'd answered the letter, made the long trip to the meeting place, and had been damn near killed for it. But no one had come to meet him. He'd every right to just pocket the money and leave. A wry snort escaped his lips. He wouldn't, of course. That wasn't his way. He'd stay to find out two things: why a pack of gunhands had been sent to ambush him, and whether

22

they'd killed whoever was going to meet him. Then he'd decide about going his way. And for now, all the questions kept returning to lovely Alicia Baxter. He had to find out more about her, he realized, and a smile edged his lips. It wouldn't be by another visit to the Baxter Ranch—not for now, at least. Alicia would have sentries posted around the clock, he'd wager. But she still fitted in somewhere, somehow, and he turned on his side, his hand coming to rest over the big Colt, and he drew sleep around himself. The questions would still be there tomorrow, he knew, but a night's sleep always helped.

The half-moon slowly made its way across the blue velvet sky, and the night stayed soft and still, and he woke when the morning sun came to bathe him in its warmth. He rose, dressed, found a stream, washed, and let the pinto drink and munch on the good brome-grass while he enjoyed a bush of wild raspberries. He moved unhurriedly, finally climbed into the saddle when the morning was half over, and took a long, circling path toward Wildcat Den. The town came into view when he reached a fairly straight road that bore marks of heavy Conestoga wheels along with a variety of smaller wagon tracks.

Wildcat Den showed its closeness to the Mississippi by the large proportion of short-haul wagons that lined Main Street, Fargo noted. He took in huckster wagons, fruit-rack wagons, Owensboro cut-under rigs, and a half-dozen Studebaker farm wagons. He slowed as he passed the General Store but rode on to slow again as he came to the dance hall. The sign over the closed doors read: THE DANCING DEN. He rode on again until he halted before a narrow building with a single window where the word SHERIFF peeled from the glass. He dismounted, and the figure that came to lean against the door wore a silver star on a flabby chest. Fargo saw the sheriff take him in with tired eyes. He'd seen the sheriff before, in countless small towns all over the territories, men who were careful to face trouble after it was over.

" 'Morning," Fargo said. "Need some information."

"Information about what?" the sheriff asked in a hoarse voice.

"About the Baxter Ranch," Fargo said.

"Take the road west till you reach the fork by the big rock," the man began, and Fargo cut him off.

"I know where it is. I want to know about it," he said.

"They raise sheep. Supply sheepherders all over the country."

"I know that, too," Fargo said. "Tell me about Alicia Baxter."

The sheriff's tired eyes narrowed at him. "I don't talk about ladies and I don't pass on gossip," he said.

"I can see you're a man of honor," Fargo said. "Now how about Alicia Baxter?"

"I'm a man who knows where not to butt in. The Baxter outfit is powerful around here, always have been," the sheriff said. "You want that kind of talk, go see Blanche at the Dancin' Den."

"I'll do that," Fargo said, and pulled himself into the saddle.

"Blanche doesn't open till after dark," the sheriff said.

"Much obliged." Fargo nodded.

"Why all the interest in the Baxter Ranch, stranger?" the sheriff called.

"I like to count sheep. Makes me sleep better." Fargo smiled and saw the resentment in the man's eyes. He rode away, veered to his right, and rode from the town, heading west toward the river as he kept the pinto at an easy trot. He had the whole afternoon to wait; he swung onto the riverbank and followed it north until he reached the bend in the river and the overhanging black willow. He dismounted, sank down onto the grass, and kept himself and the

Ovaro in full view of any passing boats. It was an outside chance, he realized, but he had the time to spare and he leaned his broad powerful back against the trunk of the big willow. A dozen boats cruised upstream as the day wore on, scows, flatboats carrying kegs and cut lumber, three arks loaded with families, one with livestock and an assortment of skiffs.

But all sailed on past him and the day finally wore to an end. The outside chance had brought him nothing. He climbed onto the Ovaro as night settled over the land. He made his way unhurriedly back to Wildcat Den and halted at the long hitching post outside the dance hall. The sound of a tinny piano drifted out through the double doors as he dismounted and followed two men into the saloon. He watched as they handed their guns to a young boy, who hung them on a wall already covered with six-guns suspended from pegs. Fargo stepped forward and fastened the boy with a hard-steel glance.

"Sorry, mister, no guns inside. House rules," the boy said apologetically but firmly.

"What if I say the hell with the house rules, sonny?" Fargo asked, his face stern.

The boy took in his size, swallowed, but clung to his firmness. "You won't be served, none of the girls will dance with you, and Miss Blanche will see that you don't stay," he said.

Fargo let his face relax and took the big Colt from its holster. "Wouldn't want to cause all that fuss," he said, and handed the gun to the boy. "Don't lose it. I'm partial to it," he said.

"Never lost one yet," the boy said, and Fargo stepped into the big room, which held the usual round tables along both sides, a bar against one wall, a sawdust-covered dance floor, and a piano player in the corner. The Dancing Den was already filled with customers, though only a few were actually dancing, and Fargo took in a battery of dance-hall girls who seemed brighter and fresher than most. His lake-blue eyes swept the room and came to rest on a big-busted woman in a yellow dress with hair almost as yellow. He saw her eyes follow him as he went to the bar and ordered a bourbon. He looked away from her broad face, which could still summon a hard-bitten attractiveness as he saw a very tall, treelike figure enter the dance hall, the smaller man with the crooked nose still beside him.

The tall man's long-jawed, narrow face focused a beetling glower at him and came toward him as the other man followed on his heels. Four strides of his long legs were enough to bring him across the floor to where Fargo took another sip of his bourbon with his back against the bar.

"You're real dumb, cousin, real dumb," the tree-like figure said in a surprisingly thin voice.

"Why's that?" Fargo asked mildly.

"Because you're still here," the towering figure said.

"Seems that way," Fargo said, drained his bourbon, and met the treelike figure's beetling stare. The man held his gaze for a moment, then turned away and moved a few feet down the face of the bar. The smaller figure, shadowlike, stayed close beside him, and Fargo saw the big-busted woman stroll forward toward him as he sauntered from the bar with another bourbon.

"Hello, stranger," she said, her voice throaty. "Just hit town?"

"Yesterday," Fargo said.

"Seems you make enemies fast," the woman observed.

"It's a talent," Fargo said. "You're Blanche, I take it." The woman nodded as she peered at him with amused interest. "Name's Fargo . . . Skye Fargo."

"Welcome to the Dancing Den," Blanche said. "The only thing that doesn't cost money here is looking." She laughed. "But you can do all you want of that."

"So long as I check my gun." Fargo smiled. "Does it really make a difference?"

"It helps. It doesn't stop fights, but it stops innocent folks from getting killed by stray bullets and my place from getting shot up," the woman said.

"Talking cost money?" Fargo inquired blandly.

Blanche's eyes held curiosity and caution. "That depends on the talk. Some talk is more dangerous than others," she said.

"About the Baxter Ranch. I'm told you and your girls hear a lot. I want to know anything you can tell me," Fargo said, and saw the treelike figure watching him from the bar.

"That kind of talk will definitely cost money, big man," she said.

Fargo nodded, moved to one of the tables, and sat down as Blanche followed and eased herself into a chair next to him. The treelike form at the bar continued to watch him, he noted. He took three bills from his pocket and put them under his bourbon glass.

Blanche allowed a small smile to touch her lips as she slid the bills from under the glass. "That kind of money will get you one of my girls along with the talk," she said.

"Maybe after the talk," Fargo said. "Start with Alicia Baxter."

"That giant from the Baxter place hasn't stopped watching you," Blanche said.

"I know," Fargo said. "Tell me about the Baxter girl."

"Alicia Baxter is one strong-minded young woman," the madam said. "She'll do just about anything to get what she wants. She was always that way, and when old Dave Baxter died a year ago, she took over the ranch. She made some fast moves with some deeds, I heard, and forced her sister off the place. They never got along anyway."

"Her sister?" Fargo echoed.

"Yes, Aggie Baxter," the woman answered.

Fargo felt the frown that came to his brow as his

mind spun out thoughts. "Aggie," he murmured. "A for Aggie."

"What?" Blanche queried.

"Maybe an answer I've been looking for," Fargo said. "Go on, tell me about the ranch manager, Ronan. Where does he fit?"

"You mean, is he managing in bed too?" Blanche said.

"I wondered." Fargo shrugged.

Blanche let herself think for a moment. "I kind of doubt it," she said finally. "Alicia's the kind that'll keep him panting so he'll do whatever she wants. I could do without Fred Ronan, personally."

"Meaning what?"

"Old Man Baxter's boys came here, but I never had any trouble with them. The crew Fred Ronan brought in after Alicia took over are nothin' but trouble. My girls don't like them either, and I keep my girls happy. They don't have to go with anyone they don't like," Blanche said.

"They seem happy," Fargo commented. "Anything else you can tell me? Where's the sister now?"

"I don't know." The madam shrugged. "I heard she's around someplace and then I heard she went away. Nobody seems to know what happened to her."

"Anything more you can think of?" Fargo asked.

"Only that it's said the Baxter Ranch figures the whole sheep stock market is theirs. Word is they've put heavy money into new breeding and selling stock," Blanche said. "And that damn giant of Ronan's is making me nervous. He hasn't taken his eyes off us since we sat down."

"He's looking for a way to start trouble and he hasn't found it yet," Fargo said.

"Bastard," Blanche muttered, and turned her attention to the big man with the lake-blue eyes beside her. "You paid for more than I had to tell you. How about that girl now?" she asked.

Fargo let his lips purse in thought. It had been a long ride with the wrong kind of surprises at the end of it. A warm woman might be just the thing to take the sourness away, and he let his eyes sweep the girls that dotted the dance hall. "How about that little one with the red hair that looks like it's real?" he said.

"It is real. You've an eye for a fresh filly. Emma's brand-new, only been here two days," Blanche said. "I'd like to see her break in with someone like you. Go over and talk to her. Tell her I sent you specially over to see her."

Fargo shrugged, drained his bourbon, and rose. The girl sat alone at one of the tables and looked a little apprehensive and uncertain, a pretty-enough face with the red hair the best feature and a small but trim shape in the low-necked green gown. He smiled reassuringly at her as he approached and drew a quick, half-shy smile in return. "Hello, Emma," he said just as he caught the movement to his right, glanced up to see the towering figure moving toward him.

"I'm taking her," the treelike shape said.

Fargo's smile was tight with grimness. The giant had found the excuse he'd waited to find. Fargo's glance went to the girl and saw the fright in her face as she stared at the towering figure, and he let a deep sigh escape him. There was no sense in trying to avoid the inevitable, he had learned a long time ago.

"The girl's mine, scum," he said almost affably.

The long-jawed face clouded instantly and a frown creased the narrow forehead. "You just got yourself killed, mister," the man said.

"Didn't mean to do that," Fargo said as his right fist came up in a tremendous hook that landed on the point of the long, narrow jaw. He heard the bone crack as the blow struck, and the treelike figure staggered backward and went onto one knee, head hanging down. Fargo saw the man look up, his eyes blink as he pushed to his feet. It had been a blow that would've kept most men down for a long count, but the giant came toward him, long arms dangling. Fargo moved backward, let the tall man come at him, and he was ready, thigh muscles tight, as the other lashed out explosively with a scooping right and a left. Fargo ducked away and felt the blows graze his face. The figure roared, came in swinging again, and Fargo ducked under the long arms and tried a left hook. But the man had a kind of awkward quickness and his body bent backward as he pulled away from the blow.

Off balance from the blow, Fargo tried to twist away, but one of the treelike arms swept sideways to crash into him with the force of a falling sapling. Fargo felt himself go down, rolled, and glimpsed the man with the crooked nose looking on. He felt the crash of footsteps, flung himself under one of the tables as a long leg missed kicking his head in by a fraction of an inch.

He sprang up, taking the table with him, and let the tabletop absorb a hammerlike blow that almost smashed through it.

"You're dead, you dumb-assed bastard," the towering figure roared, and Fargo ducked under another sweeping blow that grazed the top of his head. He sent a short, straight right out with all the power of his shoulder behind it, sank his fist deep into the giant's midsection. The man grunted, gasped as he staggered backward, half doubled over, but refused to go down. He was made of bone, sinew, and muscle, lean and rugged as a tamarack, Fargo saw, and he stepped forward, parried a blow from the long arms, and side-stepped another.

The treelike form plodded toward him again, arms held up defensively but ready to sweep out instantly. But he was still drawing in hard for breath, Fargo saw with satisfaction, and he stepped in, feinted a left, feinted a right, and threw a succession of punches with rapid-fire precision. They bounced off the man's jaw, along the side of his head, dug into his ribs, and grazed his jaw again; the tall figure stepped backward, his eyes mirroring a moment's confusion.

Fargo ducked down, came in low, tried a long, looping left that the man shook off as he lunged forward. A roar came from his throat as he reached out, tried to close long, bony hands around Fargo's throat, but the Trailsman dropped down as the fingers slid along his neck. Fargo dived hard, all the strength of his leg muscles behind the tackle. He hit the man at the knees and the figure fell back as a tree falls. He slammed into the edge of a table with the back of his head, and the table broke as it upended. Fargo heard the sharp, splintering sound of bone against wood, and a shuddered groan came from the long figure on the floor.

But the man rolled, eyes half-closed as he pushed to his feet. "Goddamn," Fargo murmured as he saw the big hand come at him again. The man's long jaw hung down brokenly and his eyes were glazed, his breath long, gasped rasps, and still he came forward. Fargo measured the treetop form as he drew his right hand back. He was about to send a final, crashing blow when he was hit from behind, a glancing blow with a bottle yet hard enough to send him stumbling forward. Through a gray veil, he glimpsed the man with the crooked nose as he went down on all fours. He tried to twist away, but long arms circled his neck and yanked him up and back. The giant's breath was a guttural sound in Fargo's ear as the arms stayed locked around his throat and Skye felt his own breath begin to grow tight. He tried to pull away, but the arms stayed locked around his neck, a death-vise grip, he realized, though the man was more dead than alive, acting out of some primitive reflex behavior. Again, Fargo tried to pull free but felt two hard blows hit into his stomach and saw the crooked-nose face in front of him. He kicked up and out with his foot and saw the face disappear as the man cursed and clutched at his groin.

But Fargo felt his own breath little more than a thin trickle of air now, the viselike arms still locked around his neck. With all his remaining strength, he dug both feet hard into the floor and flung himself backward. The towering figure went back with him, stumbled, and the arms came loose just enough for him to pull his head free. Fargo rolled to one side, came up on his feet, and saw the towering figure again lifting itself up. But the man's eyes were almost closed and the side of his head had become a stream of partly matted blood. He was actually more dead than alive, Fargo saw in amazement, yet the inner, driving force kept him coming forward. Fargo's neck and throat seemed on fire and the pain came in waves and he weaved backward as the tall form staggered toward him. He knew one thing above all: he couldn't let those long, treelike arms close around his neck again. That would be fatal. It would be a death-grip, he knew, as the last one had almost been.

Fargo weaved again, stayed low, let the man come closer. The half-closed eyes seemed to stare sightlessly; yet, as Skye moved, the long arms reached toward him. Again, the Trailsman moved backward, let the figure follow with its shuffling, almost lifeless steps. He halted, bent low, and saw the figure lunge toward him, arms outstretched. As the man's left hand reached for his throat, Fargo threw a tremendous left hook that landed flush on the point of the shattered jaw. The figure shuddered to a halt with a gargling groan and Fargo crossed a pile-driver right with every ounce of his powerful body behind it. It hit the same spot on the broken jaw and the man's head snapped halfway around. Slowly, as a tree falls, the towering figure crashed to the floor, gave a last twitching shudder, and lay still. Fargo spun and saw the man with the crooked nose racing out of the dance hall. He didn't attempt to give chase. His neck still throbbed from the viselike arms that had locked there, and breath still fought to push through bruised throat muscles.

"Take him outside," he heard Blanche say, and two men began to drag the hand's body away. Fargo turned to her, slid himself onto a chair, and drew a deep gulp of air. "You need some tender loving care, big man," she said.

"I need a few hours' rest," Fargo said, and saw Emma at his side, her shy smile filled with concern and gratefulness.

"Come," she said, and Fargo rose, followed her up the back stairs to a room on the second floor. She put a lamp on low.

Fargo saw the big bed with the brass headstand and flung himself facedown across it. He lay still and enjoyed the softness of the mattress, and he felt tugging at his boots as Emma began to undress him. He turned, sat half up, helped her as he shed clothes and finally fell back naked across the bed. Sleep refused to be denied and he closed his eyes and let the world disappear.

He'd slept heavily, he knew, aching and secure in the room, and the moonlight still glinted through a lone window when he woke. He felt the soft warmness against him at once, skin touching skin, and he turned to see Emma naked beside him on the big bed. She opened her eyes and gave a tiny half-smile that was still shy even though she lay naked as a newborn baby. Emma looked small in the big bed, and indeed, he noted, she was a small girl, but nicely balanced, breasts fitting the rest of her, tiny pink nipples on tiny pink circles, a flat abdomen, and ribs that showed perhaps a little too much. A small, slightly curved belly flowed into a small nap that rose over a surprisingly high pubic mound. Thin legs and narrow hips made up the rest of her, and her half-smile grew apprehensive as she watched him. "Disappointed?" Emma asked, and there was no defensiveness or sarcasm in the question, only a touch of sadness.

"Now, why would I be disappointed?" Fargo asked and smiled down at her. She shrugged and was happy to accept the answer. Emma reached up, drew his face down to her, and her lips opened for his mouth. Her kiss was sweet, almost tender, and he felt her shiver as his hand came up to close around one nicely shaped, small breast. He caressed the tiny pink tip and felt it start to grow firm as Emma made soft sighing sounds. When he brought lips down to the little nipple and gently sucked, pulled, let his tongue push against the tiny top, Emma's soft sighing became excited groans and her hands dug into his back. He felt Emma's back arch and the thin legs come open invitingly, close again, then fall open as her hands pressed hard against him.

He let his fingers move slowly down the flat stomach, through the thin nap, and press against the high mound beneath, and Emma gave a little squeal that was made of delight and anticipation. When he touched her warm and secret places, she exploded in a scream. "Oh, jeez . . . aaaaiii . . ." she cried out. "Oh, jeez. More, more, oh, jeez."

He explored deeper and Emma's torso twisted toward him; she drew her knees up, moving her thin legs from side to side, and her breath had become short, gasped sounds. He swung himself atop her, let his throbbing maleness touch, and Emma screamed again, her legs banging into his sides as she clasped him to her. He slid forward, and Emma's hands came up around his neck to pull him down against her, hold his powerful, smooth chest against her small breasts. She heaved under him quickly, pushed against his every slow, sliding movement, and her small form became a writhing, leaping little dynamo as she exhorted him to be quicker, harder. She cried out with her body and her lips, and he responded, plunging deep to the very end of her small, short tunnel. "Ah, ah, ah . . . aaaai . . . ah, ah, ah," Emma gasped as he answered with his own full, erect maleness, and suddenly he felt her seem to freeze, her back arched high and her nails dug into his shoulders.

"Now, now . . . oh, jeeeeeez . . . now," Emma cried out, and her thin legs held hard against him as she quivered almost in midair and he heard the half-sobbing sounds that came from her as ecstasy exploded and time froze for that instant that never comes exactly the same again.

"Aaaaaah . . ." Emma sighed as she fell back onto the bed and lay still, her small breasts lifting with each deep breath. Slowly, he slid from inside her, and she gave a tiny moan of regret but half-turned to lie close against him. He let his hand stroke her small form, caress the small breasts tenderly, and she snuggled tight and pressed the high little pubic mound hard against his still-warm and palpitating organ. "I'm glad and I'm sorry," Emma breathed.

"Meaning what exactly?" Fargo said.

"I'm glad I had this night with you and I'm sorry the others won't be like this," Emma said.

"You'll do fine. You'll learn how to pick and choose," he told her.

"I hope so," she said, and pressed against him.

He held her and felt her body relax and soon heard the soft, steady sounds of her breath as she slept. He closed his eyes and slept with her and the moon slowly moved across the sky and left the little room in still darkness.

serito horse touse. The later stop was about ah past
the water trough. Just brossed over the street and
through Main Street like the water rushes in the river

3

He woke when the morning sun filtered its way into
the room, and he rose and stretched as Emma turned
onto her side and curled herself into a ball of smooth-
skinned nakedness. In the big bed, she resembled a
little girl more than a woman, he decided as he walked
to the big white porcelain washbasin. She was still
asleep when he finished and dressed and he covered
her with part of the bedsheet. She stirred, turned, the
small breasts sweetly appealing, but stayed asleep, and
he stepped away with a smile. Emma had been the
only nice thing that had happened since he arrived. He
had closed one big hand around the doorknob when he
saw the corner of the piece of paper protruding from
under the door. He reached down and pulled the scrap
into the room, brought it up, and found himself staring
down at a note written in a jagged, scrawling script.

Go upriver. Two miles. Old Shack.

A.

He crushed the piece of paper in his hand and thrust
it into his pocket as he opened the door quietly and
left the room. He tossed a quick glance back and saw
Emma fast asleep. The Dancing Den was a silent place
in the morning as he went down the stairs and made
his way past the empty tables of the main room. Outside, the town was awake and bustling under the morning sun and he led the Ovaro down the street to the
town stable, where he bought a sack of good oats and

let the horse feed. The next stop was a short one at the water trough, and he walked the horse slowly through Main Street. But the note crushed in his pocket throbbed with a life of its own. It could well be a trap, he realized, cleverly set up to pull on his curiosity and anger. His lips grew tight as he uttered a silent oath. It'd work, he knew. He still wanted answers and he'd go, trap or no trap, but they'd find he'd be harder prey than a wolverine. He swung onto the horse as he reached the end of town.

He rode north to the banks of the Mississippi and scanned the trees behind him and on both sides as he rode. But he saw nothing move, picked up no sign that he was being followed, and when he reached the edge of the water, he began to ride upriver. He rode along the soft soil of the riverbank for a little more than a mile and then pulled into the trees, mostly peachleaf and weeping willow with a smattering of blue beech thrown in. When he came in sight of the shack built almost to the water's edge, he slowed the pinto to a halt and slid from the saddle. He took in doorless, rotting sideboards, a sagging roof that seemed about to cave in altogether, and a single, broken window. He moved closer on foot, stayed in the thick trees, and circled till he was across from the doorless entrance. Dropping to one knee, he settled himself against the dark bark of a black willow.

Fargo could play the waiting game far better than most white men. The Cherokee had taught him that waiting was simply another form of acting, and as he sat relaxed beside the willow, his eyes moved ceaselessly from the shack to the trees on both sides, scanned the riverbank, and returned to the shack. His wild-creature hearing listened for any sound out of place among the forest noises. But the hours dragged on with nothing to disturb the ordinary humming, chirping, and clicking of the wooded terrain.

The shadows of late afternoon began to slide across

the land when his body snapped to alertness. A sound had come from inside the shack, the creak of a floorboard, and his eyes were on the doorless entrance as the man slowly emerged. Fargo saw a grizzled figure with graying hair and a face that seemed to have been carved out of gnarled and knotted wood. The man carried a short-barreled carbine under his arm, and he halted to scan the riverbank. He had done a damn good job of waiting, Fargo noted with admiration, and he watched the man turn into the trees behind the cabin. The Trailsman rose to his feet, paralleled the man as he moved through the trees. There Fargo spied the horse tethered to a low branch.

The man put the carbine into a saddle holster and Fargo moved quickly, the Colt in his hand. "Hold it right there, old-timer. He saw surprise flood the gnarled face as it turned to him.

"Who be you, mister?" the man said.

"You first," Fargo answered.

The gnarled face stared back for a moment before replying. "Name's Ben Higgens," he said, finally.

"What were you doing in that shack, Ben Higgens?" Fargo asked.

The older man's face grew wary. "Waiting," he said.

"For who?"

"That's my business," the man snapped.

Fargo moved the Colt a fraction. "This says it's mine, too," he growled, and saw the older man's lips clench.

"I don't take to threats, young feller," Higgens said.

Fargo took the note from his pocket and thrust it at the man. "You know anything about this?" he asked, and Ben Higgens frowned at the wrinkled piece of paper.

"I ought to. I wrote it," he said. "You're Fargo."

"You get the cigar," the Trailsman said.

"Tarnation, why'd you keep me waiting in that damn

shack all day?" Ben Higgens exploded. "Why the hell didn't you just ride up?"

"And maybe ride into another trap?" Fargo asked.

The older man's lips pursed. "Never figured you might think that," he murmured. "But it makes sense."

"I want some answers that make sense," Fargo growled.

"You'll get them, but not from me," the older man said. "This way."

"Not so fast. I'll take your gun and that carbine while we ride."

"No need for that," Higgens protested.

"You say you wrote that note. I've only your word. That's not enough yet."

There was wry admiration in the slow smile that touched the grizzled face. "You're real careful. I like that," Higgens said.

"It helps keep me alive," Fargo said, and took the guns Higgens handed him. He walked back to where he'd left the Ovaro and returned in the saddle. "I'll follow."

The older man nodded and began to move upriver, but he stayed inside the tree line. He rode perhaps a mile until he reached a place where the river formed a narrow, tree-lined eddy that flowed back inland for a few hundred yards. Higgens turned along the bank of the long backwater eddy, rode very slowly, and Fargo spotted the figure step into view carrying a long-barreled .52 Spencer. The figure came closer and Fargo saw a young man, not much over eighteen, he guessed.

"All right, Joe," Higgens said softly, and the youth lowered the rifle as two more figures appeared, one short and fat, the other lean as a rail. Both carried muskets and the trio watched as Fargo followed Ben past. He reined up as Higgens suddenly stopped, climbed down from his horse, and motioned for Fargo to dismount. The Trailsman had one long leg pulled across the saddle as the girl stepped from thick foliage in the darkening shadows. He took in a pert, aggressive face with short brown hair, dark-brown eyes, and a small, ski-slope nose along with lips that might be soft and full when they weren't held in tightly. In a dark-green shirt and Levi's and with her cropped hair she looked almost as much boy as girl until one noticed the modest, high breasts, flaring hips, and very round, very female rear.

"Aggie Baxter," Fargo remarked, and drew a response of surprise as thin eyebrows lifted.

"How'd you find that out? You go visit Alicia?" she asked.

"I did, but she didn't tell me. Blanche at the Dancing Den filled me in," he said. "Why'd you only put your initial on that letter?"

"I was afraid you wouldn't come if you thought it was some fool girl asking," she said.

Fargo grunted wryly. "Might've made me come faster," he said. "I came, but I'm sure not happy about it so far. I want some real answers. Why didn't you show up at the meeting place?"

"I found out they'd learned I sent for you. I knew they'd be watching and waiting for a chance to get me." Aggie Baxter said.

"So you let them almost kill me in an ambush."

He saw a rush of concern flood the pert face.

"There was no way I could warn you. I'd no way of knowing which way you'd be coming."

"That's true enough," Fargo conceded.

"I kept hoping they wouldn't get you. God, I prayed over it," Aggie said.

"You keep saying they," Fargo commented. "Does her name come hard to you?"

He saw pain and anger flare in her eyes. "Alicia," she bit out. "Alicia and that bastard she hired. That plain enough for you?"

"If it is for you," he said, and she nodded with her lips thinned, acknowledging the thrust of the question without further comment. "As I was saying, I didn't know what happened and I decided to send Ben into town last night to find out."

"Figured the best place to ask and to listen was the Dancing Den," Ben Higgens cut in. "Anything happens around here, anybody found shot or strung up on the road, talk of it gets to the Dancing Den. I got there just after the fight. I heard it was between one of Ronan's men and a stranger named Fargo, so I sat back and waited in case any more of Ronan's men were there. When Blanche got ready to close, I went upstairs and put the note under the door of the room."

Fargo took in the man's words. They fitted as far as they went. "That still doesn't tell me what this is all about," he said. "I heard a few things on my own. They didn't make me happy."

"Such as?" Aggie asked coolly.

"Heard that Alicia forced you off the ranch. Is that what this is all about, family feuding? If so, you can count me out," Fargo said.

"I won't lie to you. I want to get back at Alicia but that's only a small part of it," Aggie said with a rush of determination.

"What's the rest?"

"Follow me," Aggie said, and spun on her heel. She strode away and he followed as she pushed through large clusters of branches that had been cut down and put into place. Her round, firmly packed rear moved invitingly as she clambered over old logs and pushed through more branches. When she pulled a particularly thick cluster of branches and leaves to one side, he saw the shape take form and become a large ark. A small log cabin had been built onto the center of it, and a set of corral fences were in place on the stern deck. Four horses were tethered inside one set of fences and a canvas tarpaulin covered another. A heavy Bucks County hay wagon fitted with top bows and a roll of canvas along the side took up most of the bow deck, kept in place with wheel chocks. A small, two-man skiff lay across the stern of the ark, and Aggie motioned to him as she strode toward the covered pen. She undid a corner of the canvas and flung it back. "This is what it's all about," she said, and Fargo found himself staring at a dozen lambs, the likes of which he'd never seen before.

He glanced at Aggie Baxter. "You want to do some more explaining?" he said.

"These are Orkney lambs, from Orkney sheep," she said, and he saw the slightly harsh coat on the baby sheep, the distinctly wedge-shaped head, and the good, sturdy bone structure. "I went to England to bring these back," Aggie said. "They're going to be the foundation stock for my operation. I wanted Alicia to buy a whole herd, but she refused."

"She has Suffolk and cheviot," Fargo said.

"Yes, and that's what they'll sell to all the new sheep ranchers in the Illinois, Iowa, and Wisconsin territories. But they know those breeds won't survive worth a damn, not on the land most of those ranchers have bought. They know and they don't care. In fact, they want it that way. They figure they'll make a fortune just replacing stock every year," Aggie said.

"What about the ranchers? Won't they smarten up?" Fargo asked.

"Not most of them. First, they'll take a long time to realize it's not the wrong land but the wrong sheep. Most of them don't know that much. Second, there won't be any other breeds to buy but Alicia's stock. And third, she'll have them so tied up with credit they couldn't go anywhere else."

"So they'll be hooked with her stock and nothing to do but keep struggling and replacing stock while Alicia pulls in the money," Fargo finished.

"That's right. By the time they throw in the towel, Alicia will have made a bundle."

"And that bothers you."

"Not the money part," Aggie said. "She's going against everything Pa believed. He spent a lifetime building up a name for honest dealing, and she'll ruin it. 'Never sell a man a plow he can't use or a piece of livestock that won't produce,' he used to say. 'Never take advantage of what a man doesn't know.' "

Fargo saw the sincerity and the anger in her eyes, and his own gaze went to the lambs in the deckside corral. "Just how do you figure this collection is going to change anything?"

"The Orkney sheep are an old and very unusual breed. They can survive where even hardy breeds can't. The Orkney Islands, where they were bred, is a harsh land surrounded by the North Sea. They have lived on kelp, nettles, burs, and just about anything else on the islands, and survived. What's more, they're resistant to most diseases that do in ordinary sheep," Aggie told him. "I've ewes and rams in these young ones. Alicia knows that in a year I can start selling. In three years, I can put an end to her swindling operation. I'll give the sheep ranchers the kind of sheep they can use without spending all their profits on replacement stock."

"So she's out to stop you."

"Exactly. She knew I went to England and she knew I'd bring back something to fight her," Aggie answered. Fargo watched as she reached into the deckside corral to fondle the lambs. "These are the promise of a better tomorrow, not just for me but for all the sheep ranchers Alicia and Ronan figure to swindle," she said. "I have to set up somewhere where I'll be safe and can breed and where I can reach the sheep men when I'm ready. Somewhere in the Wisconsin territory, I was thinking. But first the lambs and I have to get there alive."

"You think Alicia would kill you, her own sister?" Fargo frowned.

Aggie's reply was unhesitating. "Yes, and if she

found it hard to do herself, she's got Fred Ronan to do it for her. He sure wouldn't hesitate a second." The lambs suddenly began to grow restless, almost as one, and small, bleating noises filled the air. "Feeding time," Aggie called out, and in moments three figures appeared, including the youth who had stepped out of the trees with the rifle. But this time he carried a small pail of milk and honeyed grain and began to fill a small feed trough in the deckside corral. "This is Joe Kreiser," Aggie said. She motioned to the portlier of the other two men. "Zeke Hollander," Aggie said. "He's sailed every inch of the Mississippi. Zeke will be our captain, and Ned, there, is our poleman."

Fargo exchanged nods with the trio and fastened his eyes on Aggie's pert face. "You really figure to fool them by going by river?" he said, and she nodded vigorously.

"Alicia will expect me to go by wagon. Traveling by ark will be safer, too," Aggie said.

"Wouldn't bet on that," Fargo said.

"Amen," Zeke Hollander chimed in. "Been telling her that the Mississippi's a plenty dangerous place. Wrecked many a riverboat."

"I'm only worried about Alicia and Ronan."

"Stubborn as a mule," Zeke muttered as he strode away.

Fargo speared Aggie with a question that been gathering inside him. "Why'd you send for me? You've got a captain and I'm sure as hell no river man," he said.

"We'll have to take to the land sometime, maybe before I'm ready. I'll need you to break trail, then find a way and a place for me," Aggie said. "Meanwhile, I want you on hand."

"I don't think so, honey," Fargo said.

Aggie Baxter's pert face clouded at once. "You can't back out," she snapped. "You came. That means you agreed."

"You didn't tell me about all this shit," Fargo bristled. "I'll give you your money back."

"I don't want my money back. I want your help," Aggie said. "Alicia and Ronan scaring you off?"

"You know better than that, honey." Fargo smiled.

"No, I don't. Only fear would make a man turn down the kind of money I'm offering."

"There are a few other things." Fargo laughed. "I don't go along with fools."

"Is that what I am?" she blazed back.

"The good kind. Your heart's in the right place but your head's on backward," Fargo said. "You're going to get yourself killed over something you can't make work."

"That's not your concern. It's my neck. You just do what I'm paying you for."

"Sorry. I'm not going to help you get yourself killed."

"Principles?" she threw back sarcastically.

"You and your pa the only ones allowed?" he countered. "Call it off. Save your neck. It's too nice to lose. The odds are all against you."

"Such as?"

"First, Alicia and Ronan. I don't think you can get by them. Your sister has money and power. She's probably hired a dozen pairs of eyes and ears," Fargo said. "Second, there's no guarantee you'll make it upriver if you do sneak away. The Indians raid riverboats. So do river pirates, and Mother Nature can wipe you out anytime and anywhere. Last but not least, by the time you find a place you'll be facing winter. If you do get up some kind of shelter, maybe you won't freeze to death. Maybe you'll just starve to death. Those lambs sure as hell won't make it, so it'll be all for nothing. You'll be risking your life for nothing. Forget it. Find some other way to fight Alicia."

"I'm not calling off anything. I've made my plans. I'm going, and the lambs and I will make it, Alicia, Indians, winter, or whatever."

"Stubborn's one thing. Stupid's another," Fargo said.

"Look here, don't you talk to Aggie that way," Joe Kreiser broke in, and Fargo turned, took in the young man's smooth, unlined face, black unruly hair and deep-set black eyes. His fairly well-built body was lean and trim.

"Back off, junior," Fargo said.

"I'm not afraid of you, Fargo," the youth said, and there was only a trace of bravado in his voice.

"Good. I'm afraid of you. That make you happy?" Fargo said.

"No you're not. I'm no fool," Joe Kreiser said.

"I'm not sure of that. That's why I'm afraid. Now back off while you can."

"It's all right, Joe. I can handle things," Aggie interjected. Fargo saw the youth flash a glance at her and step backward, his face filled with glowering acceptance. Fargo started to turn away when she called to him. "Where are you going?"

"Ride out, find a spot to bed down," he answered.

"You can stay here. I'd rather you did. I don't want anybody seeing you leave by chance," she said.

"Fair enough," Fargo agreed. "I'll ride out before daybreak." He walked away and halted beside the Ovaro, loosened the cinch around the horse's belly, and took down his bedroll as night fell. He turned to find Ben Higgens watching him reflectively.

"Thought she might listen to you," the man said.

"She won't listen to me. She won't be changing her mind, either."

"It's her neck. Yours, too, I guess," Fargo said.

"Don't let Joe bother you any," the older man said. He made a wry face at Fargo's glance. "Damn-fool remark," he grunted. "I meant don't decide against helpin' her because of the kid."

"You care about her, don't you?" Fargo said.

"Worked for her pa for thirty years. Saw her grow up and went with her when she left."

"Why?".

"Never liked Alicia. She's real good-looking and real smart and she cares only about Alicia," the older man said. "Do me a favor, Fargo. Think of it again before you ride out."

"Thinking never hurts any," Fargo agreed. "Don't get to expecting, though."

"Lived too many years to do that," Higgens said, and he allowed a wry smile to touch his grizzled face. "But don't underestimate Aggie Baxter. She's got spirit and determination and she's thought about some of the things you said."

"Which ones?" Fargo queried.

"About facing winter. She figures to shoot game— young Kreiser's good with a rifle—dry the meat, and stock up on it. She's also going to store potatoes, beets, rutabagas, onions, winter squash, and grain. She figures she'll have two months before real winter comes."

"Not enough time."

"There'll be five of us, including her, working together. It'll be mighty close, but it's possible," the older man said.

"You're all staying on with her?" Fargo asked.

"I always figured to and young Kreiser's a kid without roots and anxious to plant some. Zeke has had his fill of the Mississippi. So's Ned. We'll stick with her, come hell or high water," Ben answered.

"You could get both," Fargo said, and the older man nodded as he turned away. Fargo took his bedroll into the trees and saw the lantern come on aboard the ark. He ate some dried-beef strips, spread the bedroll out, and undressed down to his trousers. Gun belt at his side, he stretched out and the lamplight finally went out.

The branches and foliage that had been put up to hide the ark brought a dark stillness to the little backwater pocket, and Fargo enjoyed the quiet as Aggie and her sister drifted through his thoughts. The ambush pushed its way in also, and he felt irritation jab at him. Maybe Alicia hadn't ordered it. Maybe it had been Fred Ronan's idea. It didn't much matter. He'd damn near been left dead along the bank of the Mississippi. He owed somebody for that and the idea of just riding away didn't sit well with him. He grunted with annoyance. He wasn't being honest with himself, he realized. It wasn't just paying back. It was Aggie. She was a lost lamb herself, taking on more than she could handle and fired by more than vengeance. She was convinced she was doing the right thing. Personal anger and missionary zeal, he grunted. The combination left no room for anything as cold as logic.

He swore softly again and pushed aside his thoughts, letting sleep come to him as the moon rose to shed a pale glow over the treetops. The stillness was a soothing song and he slept well until the sound came and he snapped his eyes open again, listened, and heard the soft creak of a deckboard. He pushed onto one elbow and peered through the leaves at the ark. The small figure sat near the bow, he saw, knees drawn up, arms around her legs. He rose and moved silently to the craft until she saw him with a moment's start.

"Trouble sleeping?" he asked as he swung onto the craft.

Aggie Baxter's eyes moved across his naked torso, took in the powerful beauty of his body, lingered on the width of his shoulders, and finally brought her gaze up to his face. "You hear me come out?" she asked, and he nodded. "Remarkable," she said. A light shawl covered a nightdress of filmy material, and he glimpsed the swell of the high, modest breasts under it. He sat down beside her and watched the pensiveness that had come into her pert, saucy face. "You're going on, aren't you?" he said.

"Tomorrow. I've waited too long now," she said,

and a glower replaced the pensiveness instantly. "And I don't want to get any more lecturing," she said.

"You won't," Fargo said. "Damn, you're the worst kind, all heart and no head. That's the kind you can't turn away from."

She peered at him and frowned as she searched his face. "You saying something without saying it?" she asked.

"Guess so," he remarked, and her frown stayed as she turned thoughts inside her. She exploded with a flurry of arms and legs as she swung around and clutched him to her. She clung hard and he felt the warmness of her slightly chunky body, her breasts beneath the shawl, and the nightdress pressing hard into his naked chest. Finally she pulled back, searched his face again.

"Why'd you decide to stay?" she asked.

"Must be feeling poorly."

"Damn, that's no answer. You said you wouldn't help me get myself killed," she reminded him. "Why'd you change your mind?"

"Decided I'd best try to see you didn't get yourself killed," he said.

Her face crinkled into a pleased expression. "I like that better," Aggie said. "And I am grateful."

"We'll talk more in the morning," Fargo said as he rose, and she pushed to her feet with him. Her hand stayed against his chest for a moment longer and she finally drew it away.

" 'Night," she murmured, pulled the shawl around herself, and hurried into the small cabin on the deck.

Fargo returned to his bedroll and sleep and woke only when the new day came. He washed at the edge of the backwater, dressed, and strolled to the ark.

Zeke Hollander, wearing a battered old captain's cap, was setting a fair-sized mast into place on the forward section of the deck.

"Been wondering how you were going to move this thing," Fargo said. "Sail, I see."

"Sail, river current, and pole," Zeke said.

Fargo turned as Aggie came out of the little cabin, a yellow shirt resting on the high breasts, her compact, firm figure with a subdued wiggle to it.

"What makes you think Alicia's hired eyes won't spot you?" Fargo asked.

"They won't be looking. They'll be watching for a wagon," Aggie answered.

"Maybe and maybe not," Fargo said. "It's plain that she's covering all the bases. How'd she find out you'd sent for me?"

Aggie shrugged. "Only thing I can figure is that she knew I was back and I'd need some help. She must've had someone watching the mail drop at the stage depot. When the letter to you was spotted, they knew what it meant," she said.

"Little things," Fargo grunted, and drew a frown from Aggie. "It's always the little things that trip you up."

"Not this time. Alicia will expect me to go by wagon, especially after sending for you," Aggie said. "If, by chance, one of her scouts sees the boat, they'll only see one more ark going upriver. The lambs will be under the canvas and I'll stay in the cabin until we're far enough away."

"They'll sure as hell spot my Ovaro," Fargo said. "I'll ride along on shore and meet up with you after dark."

"Perhaps that might be wise," Aggie agreed, and he watched Ned come along to help Zeke set the sail on a makeshift boom. She hopped down from the boat, her breasts bouncing in perfect unison, he noted, and began to pull the branches away with Joe Kreiser and Ben.

Fargo swung from the boat and helped clear away the camouflage they had erected around the ark, and when he finished, the Mississippi was visible at the end of the narrow backwater.

"We'll have clear sailing. You'll see," Aggie said to him as he swung onto the Ovaro.

He tossed her a nod and rode away as he wished he could summon the confidence that was hers. But uneasiness rode with him, pushed itself at him, and Aggie's explanation of how Alicia might have seen the letter to him only made him more uneasy. If it had happened that way, Alicia was paying attention to the little things and leaving no stone unturned. It wasn't likely she'd stop, he grunted. He slowed to watch Ben and Ned pole the boat out into the river, and then they raised the sail. It was a patched and worn piece of canvas, he noted as the craft began to move upriver.

Zeke held the tiller and Kreiser tended sail while tall Ned relaxed, his thin form at the rail, the long setting pole at his side. Aggie stayed inside the cabin and Ben Higgens moved about the boat feeding the horses and tending to various chores. Fargo stayed inside the trees as he rode slowly along the shore and scanned the thick forest growth on the opposite bank and the woods ahead on his side of the river. The Mississippi flowed quietly, the turns wide, and the ark sailed smoothly along. The river traffic grew noticeably less as they drew away from Wildcat Den, and soon the ark seemed the only craft on the river.

But Fargo felt the uneasiness ride with him as the afternoon sun rose high. He moved away from the river, rode inland, and searched out passages that led him to high ground until he found a ridge trail that let him look down at the Mississippi and the ark. But his eyes stayed mostly on the trees along the opposite shore as he rode, and he caught frequent movement in the dense foliage but nothing that formed a pattern. It was only after he'd ridden for hours and the day began to draw to an end that he glimpsed the line of horsemen threading their way through the trees that lined the far shore. They rode slowly, he saw, stayed even with the ark, and then disappeared into heavy tree cover after a few minutes.

Fargo's lips drew into a thin line as he sent the pinto downward from the high ground. Dusk had begun to stray across the river when he reached the bank opposite the ark. He frowned as he saw Higgens trailing a sounding line into the water from the bow. Fargo rode along with the boat and the old man continued to take depth measure as he raised and lowered the lead-weighted line. The riders on the opposite shore were also watching, he was certain, and he didn't dare move out of the trees as he watched the dusk darken. He grunted in satisfaction as he saw Joe Kreiser throw an anchor line over the bow of the boat in the last light of the fading day and the ark slowly came to a halt offshore. The boat disappeared from view as night descended, and Fargo reined to a halt and swung from the horse. He saw the darkness broken by the glow of two lanterns, one at the bow and the other at the stern. A few minutes later, a third lantern was lit near the cabin. He could discern only shadowy shapes on the deck and he knew those on the far shore could see even less.

He tethered the pinto to a low branch and pulled off everything but trousers and gun belt. He felt the chill of the night air against his skin as he lowered himself into the river and began to strike out for the ark. Swimming with long, easy strokes, he neared the craft and saw Joe Kreiser's head appear over the top of the gunwale, rifle pointed into the water.

"Stay right there, mister," the youth called out.

"It's me," Fargo said, and raised one arm high out of the water.

"Swim in closer, nice and slow," Joe Kreiser ordered, and as Fargo moved forward, he saw Ben appear, lantern in one hand and six-gun in the other. He lowered the lantern on a rope and Fargo swam into the small yellow circle that reached across the water.

"It's him," the older man said, and raised the lantern.

Fargo swam to the boat and found a rope ladder hung over the side, pulled himself up on it, and swung onto the deck to stand dripping wet and shivering. Aggie appeared, surveyed him for a quick moment as she handed him an oversized cotton towel.

"Why didn't you call to us? We could've come inshore for you," she said.

"Didn't want that. You've got company," Fargo said, and her eyes grew wide. "That's right," he said as Higgens and the others drew closer. "They've been riding along the other bank with you most all afternoon, maybe longer," he added.

"You're thinking they're Alicia's men," Aggie said.

"I am." He nodded.

"It can't be. She has no way of suspecting I'd be traveling by ark," Aggie insisted.

"You work hard at being dumb, don't you?" Fargo said.

Aggie's lips parted to answer, but Kreiser's voice broke in. "I told you not to talk to Aggie that way," the youth said.

Fargo turned suddenly frost-filled eyes on him. "Don't make me stop ignoring you, sonny," he said.

"Aggie hired you to help her, not insult her," Joe said, his smooth, young face flushing.

"No extra charge for insults," Fargo said. "Meanwhile, you back off. You can protect little Aggie when I'm finished trying to save her ass."

The youth started to snap out another reply, but Aggie interceded. "That's enough, Joe. Fargo's rudeness doesn't bother me," she said.

Fargo smiled at her. "I'm real relieved to hear that," he said, and saw the tiny pinpoints of anger flare in Aggie's eyes. "I'd still post a sentry for the night," he said.

"We will," Higgens said, and drew a quick glance from Aggie that held the edge of protest. "We'll take shifts," the older man said. "But it's not tonight I'm thinking about." Fargo questioned with a frown and the older man went on with his mouth a grim line. "I've been taking soundings all afternoon. The river's been dropping fast. It'll do that sometimes when there's been a dry spell or the water's backed up someplace upriver. There's no problem where the channel's deep, but there are plenty of places that are normally shallow. One of them's coming up at Cross Owl Bend. I'm thinking we'll have to cordelle her when we get there."

"Cordelle?" Fargo frowned.

"A cordelle is a towrope. It's a French word that's stayed on from the days of the early French explorers who sailed the Mississippi north. You make the cordelle fast to a cleat at the bow or around the mast, and everybody goes into the water and pulls the boat along. Where there's more water and enough manpower, you can walk a boat forward using setting poles, but where it's real shallow, cordelling's the only way and it's plenty backbreaking work."

"And that'd be the perfect time and place to hit you," Fargo said.

"And there's not a damn thing we can do about it," Ben said darkly.

"Maybe there is," Fargo said, and pulled the towel over his shoulders to finish drying himself. "When you cordelle, everybody gets out and pulls, right?" he asked, and Ben nodded. "Not this time," Fargo said. "Three of you get out and start to cordelle. The other two stay inside the cabin. When they attack, you start firing and the three on the rope dive for the bank and fire from there. You'll catch them in a cross fire for a minute or two, at least. As soon as they start to pull themselves together, I'll pour lead into them from the trees."

"It might just work," Ben said.

"If it doesn't, it will have been a short trip," Fargo

54

said. He started to turn away when Joe Kreiser's voice cut in.

"If there's no attack, if they're not Alicia's men, I'll expect you to apologize to Aggie, Fargo."

"You remind me to do that," Fargo said, and tossed the towel back to Aggie.

"You're all dried off. Ben can row you back in the skiff," she said.

"Good enough," Fargo said. "They won't be able to see from the other bank." He stepped back as Ben had the youth help him lower the skiff over the side. He felt Aggie at his side and her voice a low whisper.

"Please understand about Joe. He only wants to protect me," she said.

"I do," Fargo muttered. "That's why he's still standing upright." Higgens motioned to him and he left Aggie abruptly, lowered himself into the two-man skiff, and sat back as the old man rowed him to shore.

"The kid will settle down," Ben said. "He never had anyone to protect before."

"I think he'd like to do more than protect her."

The old hand looked thoughtful for a moment. "Could be. He's young and full of life. But he'll have to do a lot of growing up for Aggie. I know her. She'll be kind, understanding, patient, but she won't be mothering. It'll take more of a man than he is yet to get to Aggie."

"Maybe. The winter's long," Fargo said as the skiff touched the bank and he climbed out. "Watch your head tomorrow," he added, and Ben waved as he rowed away. Fargo waited on the riverbank till the skiff returned to the ark and was pulled aboard. The lamplights flicked out and he walked back to the Ovaro, put down his bedroll, and stretched out. He went over the plan he'd set out for Aggie and the others. The attackers would come racing out of the trees, but those on the cordelle would have at least thirty seconds to dive and get to the brush at the bank. Not much time, but enough if they were quick and alert. The first fire from the ark should bring down two attackers, Fargo pondered, the cross fire at least another two. The rest was up to him, he knew, and his lips thinned as he finished making his own plans. He finally let sleep sweep over him to the soft, soothing sound of the river lapping at the bank.

Morning came hot and dry. He washed at the river, dressed, and saw the activity on the ark as Joe and Ben pulled the anchor line in. Aggie was nowhere to be seen. She was still keeping to the cabin, and he grunted in satisfaction. The sail went up, hardly billowing out in the weak wind, and the craft began to move slowly upriver again. Zeke and Ned were steadily dropping the sounding line, he saw, pulling it up, taking a reading, and lowering it at once. Fargo took the pinto up a slope to high ground again and peered across the river. This time he spotted the horsemen in the distant trees almost at once and he counted twelve steadily keeping pace with the slow-moving craft.

He moved forward also, and the morning dragged on with painful slowness as the ark moved in a wind that was hardly a wind at all. But Fargo took note of the receding water marks on the riverbank and they were into afternoon when he saw the ark come to a halt and sway in the water. He could see the sandbar that rose from the bottom to stretch almost across the entire width of the river. On the ark, Ned and Ben uncurled a long, braided rope they attached to a cleat on the bow of the boat, and Fargo saw the figure step from the cabin, the yellow shirt bright in the afternoon sun. Aggie strode to the bow and followed Ben and Ned as they swung from the boat and stepped into the water, which came only to their knees. Ned walked forward with the cordelle, Aggie behind him and Ben drawing up at the rear. They brought the rope out some twenty feet, Fargo estimated, and leaned back together as they began to pull. The ark moved sluggishly through the water, and Fargo's eyes went to the far bank, where the foliage suddenly shook.

He yanked the big Sharps from its saddle holster as he sent the Ovaro down the slope, his eyes still on the far bank as the horse made its own way downward. He saw the band of horsemen burst from the trees at a full gallop, send water splashing high as they rode into the shallow river. Fargo flicked a glance to the three figures at the rope and saw them dive in unison, roll in the water, and reach the brush at the nearest bank as the riders raced toward them. Fargo reached the bottom of the slope as the first burst of gunfire erupted from the ark and saw two of the riders go down while the others reined up, started to wheel their horses toward the boat. The volley of shots broke from the brush to catch the attackers in a burst of cross fire and another fell from the saddle. The attackers did exactly as he expected they would and split into two groups, one starting to race alongside the ark, the other turning to direct their return fire into the brush.

Fargo halted the pinto just inside the tree line and swung the rifle in a short arc as he fired one deadly accurate shot after another. Three of the attackers toppled from horses almost in a direct line, as if a single, invisible wire had yanked them out of their saddles. He saw the others wheel away to flee. One turned sharply right to gallop to the nearest bank. He bent low in the saddle, but not before Fargo caught a glimpse of his crooked nose. Pushing the Sharps back into the saddle holster, Fargo sent the pinto racing after the fleeing attacker as the man raced into the trees. Fargo saw him glance back at the black-and-white horse darting after him, and the man made the mistake of sending his horse up the steep slope. The very ordinary mount began to labor at once while the Ovaro's hard-muscled, powerful hindquarters drove the Trailsman uphill without slowing.

The pinto closed ground quickly. The man turned in

the saddle, fear in his crooked-nosed face as he saw his rapidly gaining pursuer. He fired a quick shot, which was wild, and Fargo drew the Colt. He wanted the man alive and he held his fire as the fleeing horse skirted a tree, swerved right, then left as his rider yanked on the reins. The man was trying to swerve and run hard at the same time, another mistake. Fargo drew ever closer, his eyes fixed on the man as his tired horse swerved one more time, miscalculated, and swiped against the side of a tree. The rider cursed in pain as his leg hit the bark and he flew backward over the horse's rump to land hard on the ground.

Fargo pulled the Ovaro to a halt only a foot away. The man was staring past his crooked nose at the barrel of the Colt. "Get up," Fargo growled.

The man started to obey, winced, and grabbed at his leg where a stream of blood trickled from a tear in his pants. "Jesus, it hurts."

"This could be your lucky day," Fargo said, and the man frowned up at him. "You might get to stay alive." Fargo swung down from the Ovaro as the man leaned against a tree. "You got a name?" he asked.

"Kiely," the man grunted.

"Well, Kiely, you give me the right answers and maybe you can ride out of here," Fargo said. "How'd Alicia know about the boat?"

"She had us asking around everyplace. When she learned that somebody hired Ned the poleman, she figured it might've been her sister," Kiely said.

"Why wasn't Ronan with you?"

"He's got another half-dozen men watching every wagon that pulls out, just in case," Kiely said.

Fargo let a small, grim snort escape. Alicia was as thorough and as determined as Aggie. They had much in common as sisters, he mused silently. Hatred between sisters always had its own special deadliness, but sometimes a thread of affection lingered. Maybe Aggie had been too harsh about Alicia's ruthlessness.

The thought that formed inside him was worth a try, he decided, and he held Kiely in an icy stare. "I'm letting you ride out of here," he said. "You can deliver a message for me. Tell Alicia Baxter to call it off."

The man frowned back. "What makes you think she's going to listen to you?"

"Tell her she can listen and win, or not listen and lose," Fargo said. "Got it straight?"

"I got it, but I don't understand it," the man said.

"She'll understand. Just deliver it," Fargo ordered. He stepped back as Kiely rose, went to his horse, and pulled his torn and bleeding leg over the saddle with an oath of pain. The man rode away quickly, glad to be alive.

Fargo turned and let the Ovaro set his own pace down the slope. When he reached the river, he saw everyone at the end of the towrope, leaning hard as they pulled. The ark was perhaps only a dozen feet farther upstream. They halted as he rode up and dismounted, the shallow water swirling around the horse's legs just above the fetlocks.

Aggie took a step toward him, her lips tight. "She knew, dammit, she knew. How?" She bit out.

Fargo told her what Kiely had said, and he saw anger come into the dark-brown eyes and determination in the tilt of her chin.

"Damn her," Aggie muttered. "But maybe this taught her a lesson."

"I'm sure it did," Fargo said agreeably, and drew a quick glance of pleased surprise. "She'll prepare better next time." The suprise changed to anger.

"Of course, you're convinced she'll keep trying," Aggie said.

He took a moment to answer. "That depends," he said.

"What's that mean?"

"Tell you later," he said. "Maybe."

She turned away and splashed water as she strode to the towrope. Ben and the others lined up behind her, and Fargo dismounted and put his strength to the task as he grasped the rope at the end of the line. Even so, it took another full hour before they pulled the ark past the shallowest water at the sandbar. He followed Aggie aboard the boat as she clambered up the side, her firm, round rear straining her Levi's.

"No sense in you staying out of sight now," she said. "You might as well stay aboard."

"For a while," he agreed. A short gangplank was lowered over the side and he led the Ovaro onto the craft and tethered the horse on the stern deck.

Ned raised the sail and the boat began to gather proper headway. Night began to slide along the river and Fargo leaned against the stern of the boat and saw Joe Kreiser move toward him.

"You were right, I'll admit," the youth began, barely holding his surliness in, "but I still don't see any reason for talking to Aggie the way you do."

"You talk your way, I'll talk mine," Fargo said, his voice milder than his words. He turned away, aware that Aggie needed the boy and unwilling to let the youth force a standoff, which would only lead to disaster. He caught Aggie watching him from beside the corral of lambs, and he strolled to where Zeke Hollander held the tiller. "Time's going to be important now that they know where we are," he said. "Can we travel by night?"

"Hell, no," the captain said. "Only a fool would try it. At night you couldn't even see a planter."

A planter?"

"Come over here," Zeke said, and pointed out into the river. Fargo saw the tangle of branches that protruded over the surface of the water. "That's a planter," Zeke said. "The river's full of them. There are three kinds of snags: planters, sleepers, and sawyers. A planter you can spot by day. They're made of trees that have fallen into the river, tall enough and big enough to bury into the bottom mud and still reach to the surface. Sleepers stay just under the surface, entirely submerged. You don't see them until it's too late. But sawyers are the worst to me. They rise and fall with the currents and tides. You never know where one will come up, sometimes under you like a clutching hand. They can all wreck your boat, stove a hole into her, trap you so you're hung up and the current can tip you over, or spin you around onto a rock or mudbank."

Fargo nodded with his lips pursed. "I guess we sail by day."

Ned dropped anchor off the port side and the ark slowed to a halt. Bow and stern lanterns were lighted as night descended, and a third lamp was lit beside the door of the cabin. Aggie made a meal of beans and corn cakes on a grill over a small, stone hearth, and when the meal was over, Fargo put his bedroll down near the stern. The night grew still and only the soft glow of the bow and stern lanterns remained. He had undressed and stretched out when he heard the cabin door softly opened and he saw Aggie step outside.

She came toward him with a shawl around her shoulders, a nightgown underneath, and she slid down beside him, her eyes taking in his near-naked, muscled body before moving to his face. "I just wanted to thank you for being patient with Joe," she said.

"So far," Fargo grunted. "He's on borrowed time now."

"I'll talk to him. He wants to look after me," Aggie said. "There's something else. I saw you chase one of them. You get him?"

"Yes, but I let him go," Fargo said, and saw surprise touch the dark-brown eyes. "Sent him back with a message for Alicia," he added, but decided against telling her how he had phrased it. "I told her to call it off."

"Hah!" Aggie snorted, and turned a thoughtful gaze at him. "I suppose you've a message for me too."

"Same one. Call it off," he said. "Before there's more pain and killing. You haven't the cards, not for the long haul."

"You'll see," she snapped. "You'll all see." She pushed angrily to her feet and glared back at him. "I'd like a little faith and confidence," she said.

"You're paying for skills, not faith," Fargo said.

"It'd help," she insisted.

"Thought you had enough for everybody," Fargo said. "Or are you just whistling past the graveyard?"

"Go to hell," she flung at him, and strode to the cabin. She pulled the door shut with a loud slam, and Fargo smiled as he lay back on the bedroll. He'd touched a sore spot. She was more determined than confident, though she'd not admit that, especially to herself. There were plenty more troubles to come, though. He felt it inside himself. Maybe they'd change her mind, he murmured inwardly as he closed his eyes and slept to the gentle rocking of the boat.

4

He woke with the new day and washed with still-cool river water and was dressed when Aggie stepped from the cabin. The yellow shirt was open at the neck, but she seemed totally unaware of the tantalizing loveliness of the curve of her high breasts. She took a pail of feed into the lambs' corral and he walked over to watch her as she stroked each small white creature, her touch soothing and gentle, made of that special communication some people have inside them. They were more than her tomorrows to her. They were creatures to love, to nurture, woolly promises for the future. She cared, and that was her problem. She cared about the lambs, about right and wrong, and she'd let that caring push aside all logic and reason. But then reason never had much chance against emotions, he reflected.

She finished feeding and turned to him as she slipped from the corral. "I've corn cakes and coffee on," she said, and he followed her into the cabin as Ben and Zeke came up behind him. The little house was really a large, single room, he saw, with a blanket hung from a clothesline partly hiding a mattress on the floor against the far end of the room. Joe Kreiser came in and Aggie gave him a bright smile that immediately took some of the swagger out of his stance.

"You have this specially built?" Fargo asked her, nodding at the cabin.

"No, Zeke bought it from a family that came all the

way from the Minnesota headwaters on it," Aggie said, and handed him a tin mug of coffee and a corn cake.

"How long do you figure it'll take for Ronan to catch up to us?" Ben asked.

"Depends on Alicia," Fargo said.

"She won't pay attention to your message," Aggie snapped.

"Three days, then. Maybe two," Fargo said.

"There's damn little wind. We won't be making good time," Zeke said.

"We'll be fine," Aggie said, and Fargo exchanged glances with her as he drained the coffee mug and returned to the stern deck. He sat down on the stern rail and watched Zeke come out and take the tiller from Ned, adjust his battered captain's cap, and glance upward at the sky. His round face evidenced displeasure without an actual grimace.

"What is it?" Fargo queried.

"Trouble coming," Zeke said. "Weather trouble. Feel it in my bones. River man's sense, you can call it. Water's too smooth and too slow, cattails standing straight up. Something's brewing."

"Yes," Fargo agreed. "The trees are too still, the air hanging heavy, birds flying real low."

"How long?" Zeke questioned.

"Not right away," Fargo said. "It's waiting, hanging."

The old captain grunted his agreement and Ned's voice broke in from the bow with a shout. "Hard to port," Ned called, and Zeke pushed the tiller at once.

Fargo stood up and peered out into the river. The tangled branches rose up from the water as though they were a mass of clutching arms with gnarled, twisted hands waving at the end of each bony, sinewy appendage. They seemed to lean forward as the ark passed, reaching out their clutching hands, and then slowly sank back under the surface.

"A sawyer," Fargo breathed.

"Right," Zeke grunted. "Worst of all." He steered the boat back into midriver.

Fargo settled himself at the rail and watched the shore slowly move by. Aggie came outside and prepared another pail of feed and Fargo felt impatience pull at him as the ark moved with maddening slowness. He felt the itch to swing into the saddle and ride the hills, and realized why the sailor's life had never appealed to him. He felt trapped, imprisoned without bars, and he perched himself on the rail, his eyes automatically sweeping the shoreline and the tree-covered hills beyond.

He watched the land as though he were riding through the trees, and they were into the afternoon when he caught the faint movement halfway up the sloping riverbank. He peered at the land, following the movement through a stand of alders until the trees thinned, and he saw lone horseman riding slowly.

"We've got company," he muttered, and Ben Higgens came from the bow, the youth following him. "One rider," Fargo added.

Aggie came outside and joined them. "I don't see anyone."

"He's back into the trees now," Fargo said. "But he's there."

"One of Alicia's scouts?" Aggie ventured.

"Too soon," Fargo said. "Couldn't be. But he was keeping pace with us."

"He's a damn scout, all right, but not for Alicia Baxter," the old captain muttered. "He's a river-pirate scout, picking out a victim."

"River pirates?" Joe Kreiser frowned.

"There are plenty of 'em up this way," Zeke said. "Rotten, murdering, robbing bastards."

"They attack by boat?" Aggie asked.

"Boats," the captain said. "Lots of boats. Canoes, dugouts, skiffs, rafts, all small boats that let them come at you from every side."

"Spell it out for me," Fargo said. "How, when, and where?"

"They pick a spot, such as up by Swallow Corners, where the river narrows and the brush and trees come right down to the water's edge. They keep their boats hidden in the trees, and when an ark reaches the spot, they come out like a swarm of bees. They come fast, from all sides, and they're on you before you know it. Few folks survive. They all tell the same story."

"What about sneaking by at night?" Aggie asked.

"You're worse off. You can't get a good shot at their small boats, but they can draw a bead on you."

"How long before we reach Swallow Corners?" Ben asked.

"Allowing for dropping anchor overnight, I'd guess just after daybreak tomorrow. They'll be waiting, you can be sure of that," Zeke said.

"How many?" Aggie questioned.

"Usually fifteen or twenty," Zeke said.

"We can fight them off," Joe Kreiser said.

"Twenty guns against five?" Fargo put in. "And them with all the advantages?"

"Just their numbers," Aggie said.

"No, we'll be pinned down. We can't move around, hit and run, and come back again. They'll be mobile in their little dugouts and canoes," Fargo said.

"You saying there's no way?" Aggie asked, reproof in her voice.

"I'd rather go back than be killed," Fargo said.

"We're going on," Aggie snapped. "I'm not turning back. That's final."

"You afraid, Fargo?" Joe Kreiser asked, a sneer in his voice.

"Not afraid, just not stupid," Fargo answered.

The youth bristled at once. "You calling Aggie and me stupid?" he said, and Fargo smiled at how he'd quickly aligned himself with Aggie.

"Maybe not stupid, but Aggie's so hell-bent on going

66

on and you're so hell-bent on proving yourself that you can't think straight," Fargo said. He saw the youth's face darken as he started to fling back a reply when Aggie broke in.

"You're big on telling me to turn back, Fargo. How about finding me a way to go on?" she challenged. "You've all day to think about it. I don't want any more talk now."

She spun on her heel and strode into the cabin, and the others drifted away. Fargo smiled inwardly. Aggie ran a tight ship, for right or wrong, and he gave her credit for that. He settled himself at the port-side rail at the tiller near Zeke and watched the shoreline as the boat slowly sailed upriver. His thoughts stayed on river pirates and their ways. Answers continued to stay out of reach.

As the day slowly wore on and the sun moved toward the horizon, he began to think that perhaps there were no answers except to turn back or try to fight their way through. Aggie had already rejected the first as failure, and the second promised more suicide than success.

Aggie came out on deck and sat down across from him, her pert face reflecting apprehension wrapped in defensiveness. Joe Kreiser appeared and hovered near her, and Fargo returned his gaze to the shoreline. He estimated not much more than another hour to sundown. As they passed a collection of rotted logs half in the water, he saw atop them a dozen Mississippi painted turtles with their distinctive red line down the center of their shells. They were absolutely motionless as the ark passed. They'd been there all day, he knew, basking in the sun, protected by their shells from the burning rays. No other creature was so protected by its natural defense as the turtle, Fargo mused, and none so helpless without that defense. A turtle with its shell cracked or broken was simply waiting for death to arrive.

The thought idled through his mind and suddenly halted, hung there, and he felt the frown begin to cross his brow. A turtle without a proper shell was as helpless as a fish out of water. Or a pirate without a boat, Fargo murmured inwardly as the excitement caught at him and began to spiral. He let his thoughts continue to gather for another moment and finally turned to Zeke. "What happens if we moor downriver where it's wide for the night?" he asked.

"They'll stay in place and wait," Zeke said. "No reason for them to do things the hard way. They know we have to pass through Swallow Corners."

"Then we moor downriver for the night," Fargo said.

Aggie had gotten to her feet, her eyes following him. "What are you planning to do?" she asked, and Ned and Ben Higgens appeared behind her.

"Give us a chance to get through," Fargo said. "I'll need time, tools, and night. You came expecting to set down roots, a place for the sheep and for yourself. You must've brought tools."

"Yes, some," she said. "Hammers, axes, saws, mallets. They're in the cabin."

"Can't use hammers and saws. You bring a pitchfork? Awls, an auger?"

"One pitchfork, two big augers," Aggie said.

"They'll have to do," Fargo murmured, and heard the soft splash as Zeke Hollander dropped the mooring anchor into the water in midriver.

"I'll get them," Aggie said.

"No, later," he told her as he saw night push aside the twilight. "I'm going to get some shut-eye on the bow deck. It's going to be a long night. Bring them out to me at midnight."

"Midnight," she said, and he walked to the bow before there were any more questions. Ned put the bow lantern off to one side so only the fringe of its glow touched him, and Fargo closed his eyes and drew sleep around himself in minutes.

He slept heavily and the moon was almost in the midnight sky when he woke and sat up. Slowly, he drew off all his clothes except for his underwear bottoms and gun belt. Aggie was on the stern deck when he reached it, and her eyes took in the powerful beauty of him. The pitchfork and the two large augers rested against the rail beside her, and he began to push the two augers into his gun belt.

"Would you like to fill me in?" Aggie asked with a trace of impatience.

"Tell you when I get back. Meanwhile, you can pray, if you're so disposed, that I can pull it off," Fargo said.

"I think you ought to tell me now how you're planning to attack a band of river pirates with two augers and a pitchfork," she insisted.

"Very carefully." Fargo slid over the side of the craft and lowered himself into the river. He saw her come to the rail and stare down at him as he began to swim toward the shoreline. She disappeared into the darkness and he continued swimming, the pitchfork held in his right hand. When he reached the bank, he climbed on shore, rested on one knee for a moment, and shook off some of the river before he rose and began to move forward. He stayed on the bank, the ground soft under his feet, a lone figure running under the pale moon just at the edge of the trees.

He ran as the wolf runs, a long, loping gait, his body bent slightly forward, arms hanging loosely, an almost tireless pace that devoured distance and maintained his wind. He had run for more than an hour when he saw the carpet of pale silver light that was the river. He kept on, not slowing until the gentle curve came into sight and he saw two big sandbar willows that came right to the edge of the bank and hung their thin branches and frondlike leaves over the water. Beneath them, the underbrush grew thick and dense right to the water also. Fargo turned, broke off the long, loping pace, and moved into the trees. On cat's feet now, he continued toward the slow curve, grateful for the moonlight that filtered through the thick willow branches. Slowly, the shapes began to form themselves as he drew close to the two largest willows. He dropped to one knee and listened. He drew in the sounds of snoring and the shallow, rhythmic breathing of sleeping figures.

He waited, peered carefully around the perimeter of the trees, let his eyes traverse the shoreline. He spied no guards, no sentry figures anywhere, and he wasn't surprised. They'd no reason to post sentries. They didn't think about unexpected visitors. They were the ones who, when morning came, would spring the surprises.

He moved another half-dozen feet closer until he could discern the sleeping figures, stretched out in a loose circle. Their boats were positioned at the base of the circle, all facing the river. He saw two canoes closest to him: birchbark, he noted, probably taken from Indians. He crept forward to the first canoe. The pitchfork would be enough for the thin birchbark, he decided, and he pushed the sharp prongs of the implement against the very bottom of the curved prow of the canoe. He pushed the pitchfork with a quick, powerful thrust. The sharp prongs went through the bark with ease and left three small holes when he drew the tool out. They were low enough to go completely unnoticed, and he did the same at the other end of the first canoe.

Stepping carefully, pausing between each step to listen, he made another dozen small holes in the bottom of the second canoe. The next boat was a dugout, square-prowed, made out of thin strips of pine. Settling himself onto his back, he crept under the angle of the flat prow and used the auger to make two holes. It was slow, careful work, and silence was vital. When he finally finished the task, he pulled himself out from under the flat prow, listened again, and heard one figure cough and turn over. Fargo's hand pressed against the barrel of the Colt at his side. But the man returned to sleep and the Trailsman went on to the next boat. A high-sided skiff, it was sturdy once but it was now patched, the wood rotting along the planing. He used the augers to drill six neat holes into the seams at the bottom of the craft, and when he finished, he paused, cast an eye up through the willow leaves to see the moon was already far across the sky.

He cursed inwardly and turned to the next boat, almost smiling as he saw it was canvas-sided with a wood floor and frame. Using the pitchfork again, he punched a series of small holes along the bottom of the canvas where it was fastened to the floorboards. Another birchbark canoe was next, and he used the pitchfork once again, and when he finished, he lay still as he heard restless turning and coughing from the circle of sleepers. He waited until things quieted down again before crawling on to the last boat. It proved to be both the hardest and the easiest. A lifeboat from a larger vessel, it was sturdy, with the wood in good condition. But the hull was a lapstrake one, and the overlapping planks hid the holes he slowly and painstakingly bored along the bottom with the auger.

His forearms ached when he finished. He lay still for a moment and drew in a deep breath. When he rose on one elbow on the far side of the boat, he saw the horses tethered together at the rear of the circle of brush. He rose to one knee, pushed the augers into his gun belt, and picked up the pitchfork. It had gone well, he breathed with a sigh of relief; the holes he'd made were all small enough and placed carefully enough to escape detection. They wouldn't be looking anyway. They'd no reason to suddenly start examining their boats.

Satisfied, Fargo began to slowly circle the sleeping figures, moving with short, careful steps, pausing to listen and watch with each one. He was halfway around the circle when he pulled the gun belt up higher against his bare skin and the curse formed on his lips, almost gave itself voice.

One of the augers had slid out from the gun belt and dropped somewhere back along the edge of the circle. Goddamn, he swore silently. Goddamn. He couldn't leave it. He might just as well leave a note of explanation. Someone would find it, and all his work would have been for nothing. He swore silently again as he began to retrace his steps, aware that dawn was waiting to push away the last of the night. But he forced himself to move on soft, cautious steps, his eyes scouring the ground he'd already traversed. He was halfway around the circle when he spotted the tool, scooped it up, and pushed it into the gun belt again, making certain it was in tight this time. He started back in a low crouch when he saw two figures rise from the circle, stretched arms pointing skyward.

Fargo dropped to the ground with an oath as the others began to come awake. He knew he'd never make it around the circle without being discovered, and his eyes swept the scene. He needed a diversion, but not the kind that'd make them suspicious. He eyes went to the horses again and he began to crawl across the ground, away from the waking figures and toward the tethered mounts. He reached the rope tether, rose to a crouch, and made his way into the midst of the instantly restless animals. He cast a glance across at the figures and saw most were awake and on their feet. Staying hidden behind a dull-brown mare, he saw two of the men peer across at the horses.

"What's botherin' them?" one of the men asked rhetorically.

The other shrugged. "Maybe Harry forgot to feed them last night. You know how he is."

Fargo stayed behind the mare as he drew the slender double-edged throwing knife from the leather holster around his calf. With one, quick stroke he severed the tether rope and slapped the mare on the rump at the same time. The horses broke with a chorus of snorts and whinnies, one rearing half up on its hind legs.

"Somebody's at the horses," he heard one man shout, but Fargo was already diving into the underbrush. He rolled, came up on his feet, stayed low in the brush as he heard the pounding of footsteps racing to where the horses milled and snorted. "Goddamn horse thief," someone else shouted.

"Get the bastard," another voice broke in.

"Get the horses first," someone else ordered, and as Fargo crept through the brush, he glimpsed the figures racing for the animals. He kept on, moved straight for the river and away from the commotion. "You see him?" he heard a voice ask.

"Not yet but he didn't get my horse," another voice answered.

"Not mine, either," someone else chimed in as Fargo reached the river and slid into the water. He drew in a deep breath and dived underwater. He was almost midriver when he came up. The shouts still carried clearly from the shore as he let himself stay on the surface for a few moments.

"He didn't get any of the horses," a rough voice shouted. "Fan out. He's got to be around here someplace."

Fargo dived under the surface again and swam underwater until his lungs seemed about to burst and forced him to come up for air. The opposite bank was but a few yards in front of him and he swam to it under a sky rapidly turning gray-pink with the new day. Pulling himself onto the bank, he lay still and drew in deep breaths. Finally breathing normally, he glanced down at his gun belt and saw the two augers were missing. They'd slid out during the swim and gone to the bottom. At least they wouldn't be seen there, he murmured to himself and started to rise when he heard the sound of water splashing. He glanced across the narrowed river and saw the two horsemen starting to cross after him. They had spotted him as he crawled from the water, dammit, he swore silently. He'd not be able to outrun them on foot, he knew, and he stayed on one knee, the pitchfork clutched in his hand.

Keeping the implement flat on the ground, he began to back crabwise away from the river and into the trees. The maneuver cost him precious seconds, he knew, but it kept the pitchfork out of sight. When he reached the tree cover, he jumped to his feet, cast another quick glance out at the water, and saw that the two pursuers were already more than halfway across the river. He stayed in the forest and began to move away, not hurrying, his eyes seeking out thick clusters of brush in the new gray light. He found a dense clump of buckeye and closed himself inside it. The foot-long palmate leaves let him see enough to discern the two horsemen as they moved slowly into the woods from the riverbank. They separated, rode slowly, one to his left, the other at his right.

"Stinkin' horse thief. We'll teach him," the one to his right said from beneath a wide-rimmed black stetson. The other man stayed silent as he moved his horse forward, peering into the trees as dawn began to bring day into the forest.

It was but a matter of minutes before there'd be enough light for him to be seen in the buckeye, he knew. Fargo measured distance and swore softly. He could bring down the nearest with one shot, but the other one would whirl at the shot. And the man would have the distance and the time to fire. Maybe he was a crack shot, or maybe he'd just get lucky. Either way, it was too much to risk. The pitchfork would be found and they'd put two and two together. Once again, it would have all been for nothing. Fargo swore silently.

He needed that moment of surprise that'd make the man turn without instantly firing off a shot, those extra split seconds that would let him have the Colt on target.

Fargo watched the rider nearest him turn his horse in a half-circle, lean sideways from the saddle as he peered into the trees. Dawn continued to gain strength as it filtered through the foliage. Fargo tightened his hand on the pitchfork handle and he half-rose on one knee, braced his feet hard into the ground. The unwieldy tool was certainly no javelin, its balance precarious at best, but it was all he had. He lifted his arm, drew it back, took another half-second to adjust the balance, and flung the pitchfork with all his strength. He saw it waver as it flew through the air, but it held its course and the rider turned just as the three sharp prongs hurtled into him. The pitchfork twisted a fraction as it stuck: the top prong pierced his throat, the middle one entered his neck, and the third one dug into his chest just between his collarbones. The man gave a strangled sound as he pitched sideways from his horse. The other man turned in the saddle to look back. But Fargo had the Colt out of its holster, raised to fire. He pulled the trigger and the man jerked in midair as he flew backward from his horse, his chest spouting a stream of red before he hit the ground.

Fargo stepped from the buckeye and yanked the pitchfork out of the lifeless form, turned, and began to run. In moments he was into the long, loping stride, and he stayed inside the trees as the sun grew bright until he had gone almost half a mile. He veered onto the riverbank, paused to plunge the tool into the river to clean the prongs, and went on. He came into sight of the ark still moored in midriver and saw Aggie and Ben Higgens scanning the other bank where they expected he'd return. He ran noisily into the water and they whirled, saw him strike out for the boat, and put a rope ladder over the side nearest him. He reached the ark, pulled himself up on the rope ladder, and swung onto the deck, letting the water drip from him as he drew in harsh gasps of air. Little drops of water shimmered on his muscled body and he met the questions in Aggie's eyes.

"Up anchor," he said. "Time to sail." He handed her the pitchfork. "You'll have to make do without augers," he said.

"Is that all you're going to say?" Aggie frowned.

He saw the others waiting, their eyes on him, even Zeke as he hauled the small anchor aboard. "When we get to Swallow Corners they'll come swarming out at us, just as Zeke said they would. But you all wait until I give the signal to fire. If what I did works right, they'll change from swarming to swimming and we can pick them off in the water like sitting ducks," Fargo said. "Now pick your spots and stay low. We'll reach Swallow Corners pretty damn soon."

"We'll talk more later," Aggie said firmly, and strode into the cabin as the others hurried to the side of the ark.

Ben Higgens settled down near the bow, Fargo saw, Joe Kreiser taking a spot in the center of the craft, and Ned stayed with Zeke at the stern. Aggie returned carrying an old Spencer and settled herself at the edge of the cabin. Fargo, his skin all but dried by the morning sun, donned trousers, went to the Ovaro, and pulled the big Sharps from its saddle holster. He went to the bow and saw the river had already grown narrow, and he lowered himself onto the deck, the rifle barrel laid atop the gunwale.

The curve came into sight only minutes later, the big sandbar willows suddenly menacing as they reached out over the water. The ark came abreast of the first willow and Fargo's eyes were riveted to the bank of thick brush and foliage when the shoreline seemed to erupt with a flurry of activity. The small boats were propelled furiously into the water, two and three men leaping into each. They had the attack down to a science, he noted, each man using a short-handled paddle with one hand and holding his gun with the other. They started to separate as they headed for the ark, some maneuvering to come in at the bow, others from the stern. But as the boats pushed into deep water, almost halfway to the ark, Fargo saw them slow first, then come to a wallowing stop.

The canvas-covered dugout was first, filling quickly with water. The birchbark canoes were next, starting to sink straight down with surprising speed. He heard the shouts of consternation and surprise first, then oaths of alarm as the boats quickly filled. He watched the canvas dugout go under, the canoes quickly following, spilling their occupants into the river.

"Fire," Fargo shouted as he brought the Sharps up and took aim. Two bobbing heads in the water seemed to explode, and he swung the rifle, caught one of the pirates as he started to climb from the old lifeboat. The figure did a backflip into the river and sank at once as a circle of red began to stain the water.

The others were firing furiously now, and Fargo saw more frantically swimming figures go under. Two of the river pirates tried to cling to the all-but-submerged hull of the old lifeboat. Fargo took aim, fired, and one figure shuddered, thrashed the water as it slid into the river and sank with one arm still reaching upward. The second man got his own six-gun out and fired wildly at the ark as he clung to the sinking boat with one hand. Fargo ended his fusillade with a single shot, and the river pirate jerked spasmodically as he continued to cling to the boat and then slowly, almost resignedly, slid down the side and into the river.

Fargo swept the water with a quick glance and saw that it had become dull red. Some of the pirates had dived down and swum underwater, and he saw their heads come up for air halfway to the shore. Not more than six or seven, he counted, all swimming furiously to reach the bank. He lowered the rifle and rose to his feet as the ark cleared the narrow section and nosed out into the river where it quickly widened.

"Damn. You did it, Fargo," Zeke called out. "It worked like a Swiss watch."

"Seemed to," Fargo said as he put the Sharps back into its holster.

"We'd never have made it if it wasn't for what you did," Ned said admiringly.

"Sometimes everything goes off right," Fargo said.

"Modesty?" he heard Aggie's voice cut in, a trace of waspishness in it.

"Honesty," he said.

She motioned to him to follow as she went into the cabin, and he stepped inside, curiosity in his eyes as he waited. Her pert face held an edge of reproof in it, but he enjoyed the way the high, modest breasts pushed hard against the yellow shirt.

"I wanted to talk to you alone," she said. "I am grateful to you for what you did. I want you to know that."

"You afraid to say it where others can hear you?" he asked.

"No, not at all, I called you in because I thought you should've told me what you were planning before you did it. Why didn't you?" she asked severely.

"Didn't want opinions, arguments, discussions, or anything else," Fargo said.

"You're high-handed," she snapped.

"And you're stubborn and blind," he tossed back.

"I expect you to tell me whatever you're planning from now on," Aggie said sternly.

"Don't hold your breath, honey," Fargo returned. "You hired me to take you through. Not to ask your advice." He started for the door and paused, glanced back at her to see her staring after him, her face holding only stubbornness. "Nothing personal," he said, and tossed a broad smile at her. "You're really a damn cute little package."

He turned and went out onto the deck, where he saw Zeke at the tiller peering up at the sky. Fargo glanced through air that lay heavy as an unseen blanket, and he sat down beside Zeke and rested his head back against the gunwale. "It's still hanging," he murmured.

"Yep," Zeke agreed. "Don't like the feel of it. The longer it hangs, the worse it'll be, they say on the river."

"They say right." Fargo nodded. "And as there's not a damn thing we can do about it, I intend to relax while I wait." He followed his words by lying down on the deck, near the wheels of the heavy Bucks County hay wagon, stretched out flat on his back, and let the hazy sun caress his naked torso. The motion of the ark soothed and lulled him into sleep, and he dozed for most of the day. It was dusk when he woke and felt refreshed, and as he pulled himself to his feet, he saw Ned at the tiller and Zeke at the rail with Aggie beside him.

The sail was barely filled and the boat pushed slowly through the water. The shoreline had changed character and he saw a huge flock of loggerhead shrikes swooping low in the dusk. "Where are we?" he asked.

"Not where I'd like to be," Zeke said. "We're getting near the upper Mississippi, but we ought to be there by now." He cast a quick glance skyward at the gathering darkness. "I'll anchor close to shore tonight. I'm getting nervous staying out in midriver."

"Close enough to put the plank down and let me ride ashore?" Fargo asked.

The old captain nodded.

"Why do you want to go ashore?" Aggie asked.

"Stretch the horse's legs, stretch my soul," Fargo answered.

"Nothing else?"

"I'm not expecting Alicia's men yet, if that's what you mean," Fargo said.

She nodded, accepted his answer, and walked to where the lambs gamboled inside the small corral. She gazed at their small, woolly shapes with what seemed a combination of love and concern, a tiny furrow creasing the smoothness of her brow.

Fargo turned away, suddenly feeling as if he were somehow intruding, and he watched Zeke and Ned as they moved the craft toward shore.

Night settled down as the boat scraped along the soft bottom and Ned used his long setting pole to bring the stern around. Since they were moored close into the shoreline, Zeke decided there was no need to set out the bow and stern lanterns, and soon the ark was a dark bulk in the night. When Aggie went to the cabin and put on a lamp, its glow extended from the open door onto the stern deck. It provided enough light for a simple supper of dried-beef strips and beans. The meal was eaten in almost total silence, everyone staying within their own set of thoughts, but Fargo noticed that Joe sat next to Aggie, and he smiled inwardly at the possessiveness in the act.

When the meal was over, Aggie retired to the cabin and closed the door to shroud the ark in darkness again. As the others began to bed down, Fárgo had Ned help him put the boarding plank over the side and he rode the Ovaro down it and across the shallow water to the shore. He turned northward, put the horse into a trot first, then a canter. Both he and the pinto thoroughly enjoyed the feeling of space and freedom. He watched the moon rise as he finally turned around and began to head back. The almost full moon was a sphere of murky paleness, as though it were covered with heavy gauze that gave it a strangely ominous quality. The night air hung still with short, sudden swirls of wind that vanished as quickly as they came. Even the crickets were silent, he noted, and he rode slowly back to where the ark was moored. As he reached the spot, he saw the small figure on the shore, seated on a log, knees drawn up in front of her. The skiff rested nearby.

She turned and looked at him as he rode to a halt and dismounted. She was almost completely hidden under a very full, loose, dark-blue nightdress that tied at the neck with a long bow.

"What are you doing out here?" Fargo asked.

"Couldn't sleep," she said. "Something about this night. It's so damn still." He nodded and lowered himself to the soft moss beside the log. "Do you believe what Zeke says?" she asked. "About something bad hanging, waiting to happen?"

"There are signs," he said.

"And you pay attention to signs," she murmured.

"Damn right," Fargo told her. "Nature always gives signs for us to read. Trouble is, most folks don't know how to read them and don't take the time, if they do."

"What about people? Do they give signs too?" she asked.

"They give them and try to hide them. With people, you have to know how to read the masks too," Fargo answered, and saw Aggie's eyes studying him.

"What are you masking, Fargo?" she asked. "You risk your life, you come up with brilliant moves that save us all, and you do all this without any confidence in me."

"I answered that. You paid me to do a job for you, not to be a cheerleader. I earn my pay. It's as simple as that," he said.

"I don't believe that's all it is," Aggie said. "I believe you believe in me. I think you have confidence that I can do it. You just don't want to admit it."

"You want to believe that. You need help in the confidence department," Fargo said.

"I do not. Ben and young Joe, Zeke and Ned, they all have confidence in me. They wouldn't be here if they didn't believe I could do it."

"Ben's been with your pa and you all his life. He can't turn his back on you. Zeke and Ned are washed up old river men with no place left to go. You're the last roll of the dice for them. The kid's trying to get a handle on the world and a hand on you. None of those things spell confidence, honey," Fargo said.

He saw the pain inside the anger that flashed in her brown eyes. "You enjoy saying rotten things, don't you?" she accused.

"I say what's true," Fargo answered.

She turned away from him to gaze across the river, barely visible under the weak light of the shrouded moon. A quick gust of wind rippled her short-cropped hair for a brief instant, and in the shapeless garment she again looked as much a young boy as a girl. She was entirely different in looks than Alicia, he mused, but then he'd seen other sisters that were very different in looks. She turned her face to him suddenly as she felt his eyes studying her. "What are you thinking?" she asked.

"That you're your own strange combination." He smiled. "Determined young woman and lost little girl, hardheaded and shortsighted, idealist and revengeful."

"I'd rather be all those things than be greedy, unprincipled and ruthless," she tossed back.

"Like Alicia?" Fargo smiled.

"Exactly." She rose to her feet and was instantly enveloped in the billowing folds of the loose nightdress. "And I'm not a lost little girl," she snapped.

"Hell you're not. You're even lost in that dress," he commented.

She spun on her heel, pushed the skiff into the water, and climbed in. She sat down, flung a glare at him, and turned away at once. Her back to him, she whipped the nightdress over her head as she paddled away. He saw a slender, strong back, not an ounce of excess fat on it as it narrowed to a small waist and widened at once to very rounded hips. He smiled as he watched her back recede across the water. The gesture had been one of angry defiance and something more. It had said that she was very much there, under the dress, and very much there in everything else.

He saw the flurry of motion as she drew the dress back on when she neared the nearby ark, and he heard the sound of her pulling the skiff on board as he lay back on the moss. Above him, the moon continued to wear its heavy veil and he felt the sudden gusts of wind grow stronger. He relaxed a while longer and finally rose and rode the Ovaro into the river and back to the boarding plank on the ark. The horse unsaddled, he pulled the plank aboard, shed clothes to his underdrawers, and let sleep wrap itself around him in the still, dark night.

He slept soundly, and when he woke, he felt the motion of the ark as it rocked from side to side. He peered up at a sky gray as a slate blackboard, rose to his feet, and saw Zeke perched on the stern, his face drawn in as he peered northward. Fargo washed sleep from his face, donned clothes, and went over to the old captain.

"It's building far upriver," Zeke said, and Fargo followed his gaze to the far horizon where the slate gray became a purplish black that seemed more like something from the bowls of hell than a dawn sky. "I don't like it," Zeke muttered.

"That, old-timer, is sure putting it mildly," Fargo said.

'aptain' . . . she said. "And the spirit's only pull of it.
it . . . while their chosen "we . . . don't need to fly, fargo. Unless say . . . of something . . . it isn't so water

5

A red-and-black-checkered shirt with a pert face and
short-cropped hair above it stepped from the cabin.
Fargo saw Aggie take in Zeke and himself in a quick
glance and watched her face tighten. "More attention
to getting under way and less to the weather would
help," she said frostily.

Zeke's glance went to Fargo, almost apologetically,
as he rose at once. "Ned, get to poling," he shouted,
and hurried to the tiller.

Ned's tall form appeared from the bow, the long
setting pole in his hands. Fargo rose, stayed back, and
watched Ned lower the pole into the water, brace
himself on the deck, and begin to push. He used all of
his body while Zeke worked the tiller back and forth.
Slowly, the ark began to swing, bow first, and Fargo
felt the craft pull from the shallow bottom with a
shudder that ended abruptly as she floated free. Ben
Higgens came to raise the sail and a freshening wind
gave the boat quick headway for Zeke to move out
into midriver.

Joe Kreiser appeared with feed pails to help Aggie
feed the lambs, and Fargo perched himself on the port
rail, his gaze fixed on the far distant horizon and the
angry, purple-black clouds. He was still there when
Aggie finished feeding and sauntered over to him.

"The ark can weather a storm," she said.

Fargo exchanged a glance with Zeke, and the old

captain half-shrugged. "That's no ordinary storm," Fargo said. "And the storm's only part of it."

"What's the other part?" she questioned coolly.

"The flood," he snapped out. "The raging, killing flood. That storm will pour millions of tons of water into those upper Mississippi waters. First the river level will rise, and then, when it becomes too much, the river will start to pour down like a thousand runaway buffalo. It'll gather speed where it narrows and sweep away everything before it."

She looked away from him and turned to Zeke. "What have boatmen done before? This wouldn't be the first flood on the Mississippi," she asked.

"Run before it if they can, try to stay ahead of it until it loses strength," Zeke said.

"That'd mean turning back," Aggie said, and Zeke nodded. "Absolutely not," she sniffed. "What about mooring?"

"A few have gotten away with it. Most times the floodwaters spread out, lift your boat, and smash it against trees or rocks," Zeke said. "If you try mooring, you get the hell off and head for the high ground."

Aggie frowned at the old captain. "Can you be certain the river will flood?" she asked crisply.

"Not a hundred percent," he said honestly.

"Can you be certain we can't make it through the storm before it reaches floodstage?" she pressed.

"Not a hundred percent," Zeke repeated, and looked unhappy.

"Then we go on," Aggie said, and turned to Fargo. "That's called leadership," she said.

"That's called ignoring signs," he answered. "But you do have a nice back," he added.

She turned and walked away, but he caught the tiny glints of amusement that flashed in her eyes.

He went back to the rail as the boat sailed in the steady wind while Aggie had Joe help her fill three buckets with riverwater for clothes washing. He estimated they had sailed for perhaps another hour when his eyes narrowed as they rounded a slow curve.

"What are you seeing, young feller?" Zeke asked.

"Another kind of storm," Fargo grunted, and his eyes stayed on the horseman waiting at the edge of the river. He rose, and Ned came up to trim the sail and the craft slowed. Aggie came out of the cabin at once and followed Fargo's gaze as he peered at the shore.

"Ronan," she breathed. "He's alone."

"Seems that way," Fargo said, and Zeke brought the ark almost to a halt.

"Fargo," Ronan called out. "Alicia wants to see you."

"Why didn't she come herself?" Fargo called back.

"You sent Kiely back with a message. She sent me with one," Ronan said.

"That's like her," Aggie muttered.

"Where is she?" Fargo called.

"I'll take you," Ronan said.

Fargo smiled. "I'll pass on that," he said.

"You saying you won't come talk to her?" the man asked.

"I'll come talk," Fargo said. "But my way."

"How's that?" Ronan asked.

Fargo's eyes went to the land beyond the river: hills, a tree-covered slope, none terribly steep. In the north, a long ridge of red cedar topped the last hill. "Come midafternoon, she rides upland. Alone. Tell her to head for those cedars to the north," he said. "I'll find her."

Ronan's mouth tightened, but he circled his horse and rode into the trees.

"I don't want you to go," Fargo heard Aggie say.

"Why not?" he asked.

"There's no reason to," she said.

"If she wants to talk, I can listen," Fargo said. "Maybe she's decided to take my advice. Maybe she wants to make a deal."

"All she wants is to find some way to stop me," Aggie said. "She has something up her sleeve. I know her."

"We'll see," Fargo said.

"You're going to go," Aggie said with irritation. "Against my wishes."

"Guess so," Fargo said. "I play the cards the way I read them."

Joe Kreiser's voice broke in. "If Aggie says you don't go, you don't go," he rumbled.

Fargo turned his eyes on the youth and felt the dangerous irritation spiraling inside him. "You're wearing out my patience, junior," he said.

"I don't care about your damn patience," the youth said. "Aggie says you don't go."

Fargo shifted his glance to the pert face that was watching with apprehension in her eyes. "You've got thirty seconds to say the right thing, honey," he growled.

Her eyes narrowed at him for a moment before she spoke to Joe. "Maybe it's best Fargo finds out about Alicia the hard way," she said. "That way he'll remember it."

"Whatever you say, Aggie," the youth murmured, and stepped back, turned, and strode to the bow.

Aggie's voice was low, hardly over a whisper as she turned to Fargo. "I said what I did to avoid anyone getting hurt. I still don't want you to go."

"And I'm still going," he murmured.

"Bastard."

"What are you afraid of?" Fargo asked. "You know I'm not about to let myself be trapped. What else are you afraid of?"

"Nothing. Absolutely nothing," she snapped, and stalked into the cabin.

Fargo turned to Zeke, who shrugged. "Move inshore when we're past that ridge of cedars," the Trailsman said.

Ben Higgens moved to stand beside him at the port

rail. "You have to understand Aggie. She won't deal with anyone she considers impossible to trust, and she doesn't want you to either," Ben said.

"It's more than that," Fargo answered. "It's got a special edge."

"Maybe she just knows Alicia too well." Ben shrugged.

"Maybe," Fargo said, and remained unconvinced. When the ark finally began to draw abreast of the distant line of red cedars, he saddled the Ovaro and was ready when Zeke moved inshore. With Ned working the setting pole, he maneuvered tight into shore and Ben lowered the boarding plank. Fargo took the Ovaro down the plank and into the shallow water and turned to see everyone but Aggie at the rail.

"You want us to wait for you?" Zeke asked.

"Hell, no," Fargo said with a grim glance at the distant sky. "There's no time for waiting. I'll catch up to you when I'm ready."

"Good luck," Zeke called, and Ned pulled the plank in.

Fargo rode through the water to the riverbank and into the trees. He headed up the slopes at once and let the pinto run hard and free, slowing only when he finally reached the crest of the first hill. He let the horse rest a moment, blow out air, and then he moved on across the next hill. His eyes swept the terrain as he rode, the habit as much a part of him as his skin. This was mostly Sauk Fox, Kickapoo, and Winnebago country, but the Iowa and the Ojibwa strayed over, and when they did, they were looking for trouble. But he saw nothing to alarm him, and when he finally neared the top of the hills, he turned the horse east and put the line of cedars to his left. He found a small plateau that let him look down on the entire hillside and he relaxed in the saddle as his eyes moved ceaselessly back and forth.

The hills were long and heavy with tree cover, and

he didn't waste time and energy trying to pick out a lone rider. Instead, he watched the movement of branches and leaves, distinguishing as only he was able the small, subtle differences between the ways of wind and the ways of bird, beast, and man. Almost an hour had passed before he spotted the movement at the center of the slope, the unmistakable pattern of horse and rider proceeding upward. He waited, watched as the rider came closer, and then shifted his gaze to the land just beyond. His eyes narrowed and he grunted with grim cynicism as he spotted the motion that revealed a second horseman following.

He moved the Ovaro forward, turned, and headed for a place on the hillside where lightning had once struck and the fire cleared a ragged circle. Three tall boulders jutted up at the edge of the blackened ground where only saplings grew. He moved the horse behind the rocks as he waited. He slid from the saddle, the big Sharps in his hand, and it was perhaps another fifteen minutes when he glimpsed the horse and rider slowly weaving in and out of the trees at the edge of the charred clearing. He saw Alicia's black hair hanging loose around her shoulders as she sat a brown gelding. She wore a white shirt and dark blue Levi's and glanced nervously right and left as she rode. Fargo continued to wait, and as he shifted his gaze to the thick tree cover some twenty-five yards behind her, he saw the foliage rustle.

He looked back at Alicia and stepped halfway from behind the rocks as she neared the end of the clearing. "Over here," he called, and saw her start in surprise. She reined her mount in and turned toward the rocks. Carrying the rifle against his waist, the barrel held straight at her, he stepped completely from behind the rocks.

Alicia halted her horse and faced him with her thin black brows faintly arched. "You don't need that," she said.

Fargo's eyes went past her where the leaves quivered in the distance. The horse and rider came into view for a brief instant. The rifle, already all but on target, shifted a fraction of an inch, and the single shot exploded in the stillness of the blackened clearing. Fargo saw the horseman half-rise out of the saddle and spin before he toppled backward into the brush with a very audible crash.

Alicia spun in the saddle to stare back into the trees and Fargo saw the astonishment flood her face.

"I told you to come alone," he said coldly.

"I didn't know he was there," Alicia said. "I didn't know I was being followed. Fred must've sent him after me."

Fargo peered hard at her. The surprise seemed genuine enough. Perhaps she was being truthful, he mused. Perhaps. "Fred should've listened to me," Fargo commented.

"I guess so," Alicia said, and frowned at him as she nodded toward the distant trees. "Maybe he was just there to look after me. Fred said it was dangerous to ride Indian country."

"I said come alone," Fargo growled.

"You could have waited some before you fired."

"Waiting can get you dead."

Her dark-brown eyes appraised him with something between wariness and admiration. "You're everything they say about you, aren't you?" she remarked.

"Maybe," Fargo grunted.

Alicia Baxter swung down from her horse, her long figure moving with supple grace. Her breasts pressed tight against the sides of the white shirt, and her pale-white skin and firm litheness gave her a combination of delicacy and strength. "I've thought about the message you sent me," Alicia said, taking a few steps toward him. "You obviously feel that little Aggie can't carry it off." She offered a cool smile and he let silence be his answer. "You're right, of course," Alicia said. "Then why are you wasting time and effort helping her?"

"I think she deserves a chance, and I've been lied to, bushwhacked, and attacked. That makes me sort of bothered," Fargo said.

"Fred gets carried away with himself. He makes a lot of stupid mistakes," Alicia said, her tone becoming soothing. She was glib at casting everything on Ronan's shoulders, he reckoned.

"You say she can't carry it off. Why are you so busy trying to do her in?" Fargo questioned.

"I can't take the chance that she might get lucky. I've too much invested in this to risk that," Alicia answered.

"You saying you won't back off?" he pressed.

"I can't," Alicia said. "But I just want to stop her. That'd happen if you weren't along with her. I'm convinced of that. We met what was left of those river pirates. They told us what happened. You did it, just as you smashed the attack by Fred's men."

"I wasn't alone," Fargo said.

"Don't play games with me. It sure wasn't that kid or that collection of has-beens little Aggie has put together," Alicia said chidingly. Her voice softened and she stepped closer to him, dark-brown eyes peering up at him, and he smelled the faint odor of powder and perspiration mingled together in a musky, softly exciting scent. "Come in with me. I can use someone like you," she said. "And without you, Aggie will find she just can't make it and she'll give up."

"You know better than that, honey," Fargo said.

"She won't have any choice."

"She'll keep trying and die for it," Fargo said. Alicia's shoulders lifted as she shrugged. "That doesn't even bother you a little?" Fargo questioned.

"I've no patience with fools, and Aggie's always been a fool. Her head's always been full of starry-eyed notions and romantic ideals," Alicia said disdainfully.

"Is that the stuff of fools?" Fargo smiled.

"Yes," Alicia snapped, and studied him again with a long glance. "You're a realist," she said. "You belong with me."

"You have a right-hand man," Fargo mentioned.

"One who's been doing too many dumb things," Alicia said crisply. "You come in and he's out. You'll make a lot more money with a lot less effort than you ever will with Aggie."

"Sometimes it's more than money that keeps a man around." Fargo smiled.

Alicia let her lips purse and her dark-brown eyes took on a hint of smoky amusement. "You won't be getting anything but money from Aggie," she said.

"You saying I'd get something more from you?"

She took the question with a tiny smile edging her full, red lips. "Maybe."

"Maybe doesn't cut much ice with me, honey."

Alicia's little smile stayed in place. "You be more definite, and so will I," she returned.

"I'll have to think some."

"Not too long, I hope," Alicia told him. "I've never liked waiting."

"Tomorrow," he said.

"Where?" Alicia asked.

"You and the others will be keeping pace with the ark," Fargo said. "You ride higher on the hills, apart from the others. I'll do the rest."

She took a step closer and her hand rose, circled around the back of his neck, and she reached up and pressed her lips to his, a soft kiss that lingered for exactly the right length of time to tantalize, a kiss both proper and promising. "That's to help you think," she murmured when she pulled back. She swung smoothly onto the brown gelding, her rear a small, tight mound under narrow hips.

"You can find your way back?" Fargo asked.

"Straight down the hills," she said, and rode slowly away.

Fargo watched her ride downhill and saw the riderless horse appear and follow behind her. When they were both out of sight, he climbed onto the pinto and cut a path to the right and then downhill. Alicia was smooth and very close to beautiful, and the taste of her lips still clung. She was also completely in control of her every move. While Aggie was pugnacious stubbornness wrapped in anger, Alicia was icy determination wrapped in quiet ruthlessness. She'd tossed blame off on Ronan's shoulders, but Fargo felt there wasn't anything that went on in her operation she didn't know about. But he'd bought another day, and maybe, just maybe, he could still get her to bend some. He spurred the pinto forward and hurried down the hill.

Dusk was turning into dark when he reached the riverbank and rode north until he spotted the ark moored close inshore. He rode the pinto into the water, and the boarding plank was lowered when he reached the boat with the horse in water up to his brisket. "You come inshore for me?" he asked when he was on board and the plank pulled up.

"No, current's running too fast to moor midriver," Zeke said. "We'll take sentry shifts for the night."

"No need to for tonight. Things are on hold," Fargo said.

"We'll post sentries," Aggie's voice cut in. "I haven't been sweet-talked into being a damn fool."

Fargo smiled at her and saw she wore the loose, enveloping nightdress. "Me neither, honey," he said, and walked after her as she strode into the cabin and put a lantern on.

"You didn't talk about the weather with her," Aggie snapped, acid clinging to each word.

"Not exactly," Fargo admitted.

"She offered to pay you to get me to quit," Aggie said, her chin tilted upward defiantly.

"Something like that," Fargo answered carefully, trying not to let the wrong words stir more fury in her.

"What'd you say? You tell her you'd try?" Aggie speared.

"I told her I didn't have enough influence for that," he said placatingly.

"That's for damn sure," Aggie grumped. "What else did she have for you?"

Again he picked out words with care. "Money. She offered me money," he said. "Money didn't count for that much, I said."

"And she offered something more, of course."

He kept his face expressionless as she searched his countenance. "Wouldn't say that," he replied. "But she said that money was all I'd ever get from you."

"Bitch."

"You telling me she was wrong?" he asked blandly, and drew instant fire from her eyes.

"No," she snapped. "I'm telling you that's exactly the kind of thing she'd say. What else did she have to say?"

"We agreed to talk again tomorrow," Fargo said.

"No, absolutely not," Aggie almost shouted. "You go to see her again, and you needn't bother coming back."

"What are you so damned afraid of?" Fargo frowned.

"Nothing," Aggie flung back. "I'm not afraid of a damn thing. There's just no point in you seeing her again."

"Unfinished business. Maybe I can still convince her to back off," Fargo said. "It's worth another try."

"You won't. I know Alicia, the way she thinks and acts. You just stay away from her or don't come back," Aggie repeated.

Fargo studied her, peered hard into her eyes, and she turned away quickly. More than anger, he told

94

himself again. He'd caught a glimpse of something that was almost pain inside the fury. He decided not to answer, and walked from the cabin. He heard the door slammed shut behind him as he went to the Ovaro and put his bedroll down on the stern deck. He undressed and stretched out, aware that the soothing, slow rock of the boat had become a deep swaying motion that tugged at the mooring line. But he slept in the warm wind that blew almost without stop now, and the night finally passed into morning.

He woke and felt the wind against his body at once, hot and damp, a fervid quality to it. He washed and dressed, and when he finished, he saw Zeke and Ben appear to huddle together at the rail.

Zeke looked up as Fargo approached. "Rising too fast and running too strong," the old captain said. "We'll be making damn little headway today."

In the distance, the purple-black storm sky continued to hang. It was pouring rain down into the upper Mississippi, he knew, and felt his lips tighten.

Ned came to help pull the anchor up and Zeke took the tiller as Ben raised the sail and the ark was swept out into midriver, spinning around until Zeke got the bulky craft under control. The water slapped hard against the prow as the boat slowly moved forward despite the fullness of the sail.

Aggie came out with a wooden tray of coffee mugs, refusing to meet his eyes as she paused beside him. He took a mug as Joe Kreiser came up and took the tray from her solicitously as she almost lost her footing when the boat swayed hard to port.

"Damn," Zeke muttered while he pulled hard on the tiller and the craft swung about on course again. Aggie fed with lambs with Joe after everyone finished coffee, and Fargo waited and watched the shore, but he saw no horsemen. Ronan was keeping his men up on the hills and in the trees, and Fargo let most of the morning go by before he went over to Zeke.

"Can you get inshore some?" he asked. "I'm going riding."

"I can do it, but you'll have to get down the plank fast," Zeke said, and Fargo nodded, strode to the Ovaro, and saddled the horse. Aggie came out of the cabin the minute she felt the boat moving to shore and slowing its forward motion.

Fargo waited beside the pinto, one hand resting on the saddle horn while Zeke peered at the waters. "There," he said, pointing to a patch of relatively calm water. "Over that sandbar." He steered the boat toward it while Ben Higgins began to lower the boarding plank. Fargo swung onto the Ovaro and met Aggie's eyes.

"Damn you, Fargo," she hissed. "I meant what I said last night."

"That was last night," he said as he spurred the horse to the plank.

"I mean it this very minute too," she shouted.

He cast a quick glance at her and sent the horse down the plank and into the water with a splash. When he reached the bank and pulled out of the water, he looked back and saw the ark already back in midriver, Aggie a small figure, her hands clenched against the rail. He saw Joe Kreiser go to her side and take her arm with protective sympathy. The youth would be the real problem, sooner or later, Fargo murmured to himself as he swung the Ovaro up into the higher ground. He headed south first, then turned uphill and doubled back when he was almost at the top line of the slope. He rode parallel to the river below, visible only in brief glimpses where the trees broke.

He'd gone some half-hour when he spotted the horsemen below near the bottom of the hill, and he frowned. There were considerably more than he'd expected. They were moving in and out of the heavy tree cover too quickly for him to make a count, but he guessed there had to be at least twenty. His eyes moved up toward the center of the slope and he finally spotted Alicia, the white shirt a pale flash as she moved through the trees. His eyes swept the land behind her and in front of her. Finally satisfied that she was alone, he moved the Ovaro downward at an angle that brought him close to her. He picked out a short passage of thick grass and chickweeds that grew heavily and came up to her in silence. "Rein up, honey," he said softly, and she jumped in surprise and fright, then pulled the horse to a halt. He came out from the trees, and her eyes studied him from beneath the thin black eyebrows.

"You are good." she remarked.

"That's how I stay healthy, he said.

She swung in beside him as he turned and began to climb again. He'd make her play her hand out and he wanted the right place for her to do it. As he moved upward, his lake-blue eyes narrowed, and scanning the terrain, he glimpsed a flock of Baltimore orioles swoop downward to disappear beyond a growth of shagbark hickories. He followed the flight of the birds and rode higher into the hillside to push through the hickories. When he reached the far edge of the trees, he saw the small rectangular pond ringed by a carpet of mountain fern moss and a circle of young willows.

He halted, swung down from the horse, and walked onto the soft moss. He watched Alicia dismount with one graceful motion, and he lowered himself onto the moss with his hands behind his head. He felt her eyes move up and down his perfectly proportioned body wiht appreciative leisure.

"You think about my offer?" she asked, and sank down beside him.

"I thought," he said laconically.

"I hope you decided right," Alicia said, a toying quality in her tone.

"I decided talk is cheap," Fargo murmured.

Alicia's smile held the anticipation of triumph in it. "Would you make your mind up if you had more than talk?" she asked.

"It'd sure help," he said blandly.

Alicia leaned forward. "Well, I do want you to make up your mind," she said. "The right way."

He stayed unmoving as her lips came down on his, soft at first, then growing stronger, pressing, moving to open wider. She pulled back and he watched her hand move to the buttons on the white shirt. She opened them slowly, tantalizingly, and a little smile curled her lips as she enjoyed his eyes on her. When the blouse hung open, she made a quick, wriggling motion with her shoulders and it came off, and he saw longish breasts that turned very full at the bottoms, each round cup centered with a bright-pink tip on a paler-pink circle. She stretched her legs out and, wordlessly, opened the Levi's, pulled off undergarments and pants at once, and rose onto her knees naked in front of him. A long, slender body, he saw, ribs showing when she breathed in, a flat belly, and a very inky, dense, compact triangle. Narrow hips and slender legs, everything of the same pale, delicate white skin that emphasized the blackness of the triangle and the bright pink of her nipples.

"Very nice," Fargo said. "Damn nice."

Alicia smiled, leaned forward, and began to unbutton his shirt. He helped her pull off gun belt and Levi's, and when he was naked before her, she devoured him with her eyes. "Damn nice," she echoed. "Exceptional, to be truthful." Her hands came up, pressed against his chest, moved slowly down in a sliding motion, passed the hard flatness of his abdomen, and reached to where he was already throbbing with excitement and wanting. "Oh, Jesus," Alicia breathed as she clasped her fingers around him. "Oh, give me, Jesus, give me." She pulled gently and he went with her, came against her and pressed her back onto the moss and lay atop her, his maleness pressed into the compact triangle.

Alicia cried out at the touch of him and he felt her slender legs fall open, lift at once to press against his sides. His hips were moving, swaying from side to side, and her hands clasped behind his neck to pull him toward her.

He held back, let her lift, her torso shifting to one side and then the other as she sought him with her waiting warmness. He put his mouth down over one bright-pink nipple, sucked gently on it, and Alicia gave a short, gasped cry of delight. But her hips continued to move under him, seeking, demanding, the flesh crying out for flesh.

He let his fingers travel down her slenderness and she cried out again and lifted hips. He closed his hand against the dark and secret place, and Alicia let a groan of desire escape her. She was moist, warm wetness flowing in eagerness, and her hands dug into his shoulders. "Give me, damn, give me," she whispered almost savagely, and pushed upward with legs and hips. There was no time for subtlety or lingering pleasures with Alicia, he realized, and he felt her haste had the tinge of impatient calculation in it. He brought his body around, let his maleness swell forward, and pushed into the moistness of her warmth.

"Ah, ah, Jesus," Alicia cried out, and there was only raw pleasure in the sound. "Yes, yes, dammit, oh, yes," she breathed as he pushed deep, drew back, and pushed again. Her hips lifted to meet his thrusting movements. "More, more, oh, yes, oh, yes," Alicia demanded, her voice breathy, but there was no longer any calculation in her, the haste made of the flesh wanting ecstasy, the body responding to its own desires.

He went with her, thrusting deep to meet her surgings, and he felt the wet warmth of her, the language of flesh and wanting. Alicia continued to cry out little sounds of demand, and he responded, quickened his thrusting, drawing back and plunging deeply each time until suddenly he felt her breath draw in. "Ah, ah . . . ah, now, now, come with me, dammit, come with me," she cried out, her voice rising, becoming a half-scream.

He let himself go, felt the gathering inside him as her slender legs squeezed around his waist and the longish breasts fell from side to side as her torso twisted furiously. He exploded with her and she screamed, a sharp, piercing cry, a strange sense of relief mixed with release in it, and when she fell back onto the carpet of moss, she made little mumbling sounds. He stayed with her, moved slowly, and enjoyed the sensation of the embers of passion, but Alicia pushed backward. "That's enough," she murmured, and he slid from her and saw her eyes peering at him with a strange, almost hostile burning. She blinked; the moment passed and she sat up, stretched, and let him enjoy the long slender beauty of her, breasts swaying gently as she half-turned and reached for the Levi's. She pulled on undergarments, Levi's, and her shirt, and he rose and began to dress. She leaned back on her palms as he put his gunbelt back on and then his shirt, her glance speculative, the tiny smile back on her lips. "That help you make up your mind?" she asked.

"It sure did." Fargo smiled and pulled her to her feet. "I kept wishing you were doing this because you were wanting instead of selling."

Alicia's eyes narrowed instantly. "What's that supposed to mean?" she murmured.

"You were trying to sell me, not screw me," Fargo said. "You were pussy-bargaining, honey. It helped me make my mind up, though. I'm going to stick it out with Aggie."

"You bastard," Alicia rasped, and her loveliness was suddenly frozen fury.

"Maybe I won't get anything more from Aggie, but whatever I get will be real," Fargo said calmly.

"You tricked me," Alicia spit at him.

"You wanted to help me make up my mind, and you did. You tried something that didn't work. You tricked yourself, honey."

"Son of a bitch," Alicia shouted, and her hand came up in a short arc, fingers outstretched to rake his face with her nails.

Fargo pulled back, caught her wrist as the blow grazed him, and spun her around. She yelped as he pulled her arm up behind her back. He brought his other hand up and caressed her breasts as she cursed.

"You ought to learn to enjoy these, not use them, Alicia," he said, and flung her away from him. She stumbled forward against the brown gelding and grabbed hold of the saddle horn to keep from falling. Her eyes were pinpoints of rage as she looked back at him.

"You'll pay for this, you bastard," Alicia said, and pulled her long body into the saddle.

Fargo started to turn away when he saw her reach into the saddlebag. He was whirling, dropping into a crouch as her hand came out holding a small, short-barreled rimfire pistol. She fired three shots into the air, and Fargo, the Colt already in his hand, dropped the gun back into its holster as Alicia galloped off into the trees. The three shots were an alarm signal, and Ronan and his posse were already charging up the hillside.

He spun, leapt onto the Ovaro, and sent the horse racing north across the slope. He knew Ronan would have his men spread out as they raced uphill, and Fargo continued north across the center of the slope. He slowed when he heard the sounds of horses coming toward him from below. Spotting a dense cluster of black oak, he rode the Ovaro into the trees, slid from the saddle, and moved on foot to the edge of the thick oak grove. Two horsemen came into sight, moving quickly through the trees. They were some ten yards apart and shots would only bring the others racing back, he knew. He stayed low and drew the thin, double-edged throwing knife from its calf-holster around his leg. He brought the blade up, watched the men draw closer. One pulled ahead of the other and made a half-circle to the left. Fargo let the second one draw still closer, raised his arm, measured distance, movement, and the strength of the hot wind that blew through the forest. The man was almost facing him when he flung the blade, a short, overhand throw that sent the thin blade hurtling through the air with the force of an arrow.

It sank into the man's chest even as his eyes widened as he saw it, embedded to the hilt. The man's eyes continued to widen, his mouth opened in a soundless cry, and he clutched the handle of the knife with both hands in a futile attempt to pull it out. His hands were still on the handle as he started to topple from his horse. But Fargo was racing forward and caught the figure before it hit the ground. He held the man in his grip for a moment and then lowered him quietly to the ground. He stayed low, on one knee, behind the horse and heard the first rider call out. "Akins?" the man shouted.

Fargo muffled his voice with one hand. "Over here," he called back. "Got somethin'." He heard the other horse being turned at once, and the man rode over at a canter. The throwing knife was too deeply embedded in its target, and Fargo drew his Colt. As the first man reined up, he leapt out from beneath the horse, dived up and forward, and saw the man try to draw his own gun. Fargo smashed the barrel of the Colt into his face, ducked away from the gusher of red that erupted as a deep gash opened between the man's eyes and his broken nose. He heard the man gargle an oath, clutch at the saddle horn to keep from falling, but Fargo took hold of one leg and yanked and the figure fell from the horse. Fargo brought the barrel of the Colt down again, atop the man's head this time, and the figure half-rolled over and lay still.

Fargo waited in a crouch, listened, and heard only the sounds of distant horses moving through the forest. He turned, grimaced as he pulled the throwing knife free and wiped the blade clean on a patch of bromegrass. He brought the Ovaro out of the oaks and rode northward again. But he'd gone only a few hundred yards when he spotted the second set of riders moving uphill ahead of him, and he turned, searched the woods, and found a collection of fallen trees, many split by lightning, leaning across one another behind thick foliage. They formed a kind of rotting bower and Fargo took the Ovaro inside it, dismounted again, and waited with the Colt in hand. He heard the horsemen pass, glimpsed three, and guessed there were at least six. Ronan had a second group riding upriver ahead of the arc apparently, and Fargo stayed inside the hiding place as he heard the riders circle. He heard others draw close and hurry on. Ronan had his men scouring the woods, swarming antlike in all directions, but they were all moving too fast, his ears told him, all amateurs mistaking activity for progress.

He decided to stay in the hiding place and not risk another confrontation, and he finally heard them move on, make a few more passing sweeps, and ride away. But he stayed until he felt the day drew to an end, the hot wind begin to cool, and the gray skies darken. He led the Ovaro out of the ragged bower, took to the saddle, and rode at a walk, listening with every few yards. But the search had been called off, and he started to move downhill as he rode north.

Night seeped down through the trees, and the moonless dark shrouded the earth as he neared the river. He heard the sound of fast-moving water first and halted when he emerged onto the bank to see that the Mississippi had become a dark, angry ribbon of rushing water that bounced and sprayed high along the shore. He rode on, rounded a small bend, and spied the ark moored inshore, perhaps a half dozen yards from the bank. A faint glow came from inside the open cabin door to light the rear deck, and Fargo spotted Ben and Zeke by the rail. He sent the Ovaro along the shore upriver from the boat before he turned into the water. The swift-moving current caught at the Ovaro at once and swept the horse downriver. When it neared the ark, Fargo turned the pinto, brought his palm down on the horse's rump, and felt the Ovaro's powerful legs strike out for the ark. Fargo saw Zeke and Ben spot him and rush to put down the boarding plank just as the Ovaro reached the side of the boat. Fargo slid into the water and let the horse pull himself onto the plank without the weight of a rider, held on to the pinto's saddle strings, and found his own footing on the plank. He half-stumbled up beside the pinto as the horse pulled itself out of the water and onto the boat. And Fargo fell to one knee and drew in a deep breath.

Zeke and Ben pulled the plank up and Fargo rose, shook water from himself, pulled his shirt off, and draped it across the rail. "Gave you up for gone," Zeke said.

"Not yet," Fargo grunted, and saw the figure in the open doorway of the cabin, close-cropped hair framed by the lamplight behind her. She wore a shawl over a bare-shouldered nightgown, he saw, and her brown eyes bored into him.

"What are you doing here?" Aggie snapped. "You know what I told you before you left."

"I've got a terrible memory," Fargo said.

"Well, I've got a good one."

"Inside," he growled as he strode past her.

She was on his heels as he entered the cabin and she pulled the door shut. "You get off this boat, Fargo," she said angrily as he turned to face her. "I don't want you here. I don't need you. I'll go it alone."

"Stop being a damn fool altogether," Fargo barked.

"I don't want your help, not after you've been with her."

Fargo let the frown crease his brow. "What's that mean?" he questioned.

"You know what it means," Aggie said stiffly.

The frown dug deeper. "No, I don't. Spell it out," he said.

"You slept with her," Aggie threw at him, and Fargo had an effort to keep surprise from his face.

"Now, what in hell makes you say that?" he asked, keeping his voice casual as surprise continued to curl inside him.

"I just know it," Aggie said, and sounded suddenly like a hurt little girl.

"You're fishing," Fargo said.

"I am not. I *know*," Aggie replied. "It's her way. It's always been her way."

"Always been her way?" Fargo echoed.

Aggie turned from him, her hands clenched, and he saw her try to stop her lips from quivering. "She did it with every boy that came to see me," Aggie said, her voice wavering. "She'd give herself to them, sleep with them, just to take them from me. Later on she'd throw them away."

"And of course you wouldn't have anything to do with them then," Fargo said.

"Of course not," Aggie snapped indignantly. "Besides, they never came back."

"You ever think of doing the same thing to Alicia and taking her boyfriends?" Fargo asked.

Aggie wiped a hand across her eyes and he saw the remembered pain there as she looked at him almost reproachfully. "How could I compete with her looks? How could I take one of her boyfriends? There was no way, and she enjoyed not letting me have the ones that came to see me. I'll always hate her for that, and now she's done it again. I knew she would."

"I came back. I'm here," Fargo said.

"Yes, you're here, but I wonder why."

"You paid. I promised. I keep my word."

Aggie stared back for a moment. "But you slept with her, didn't you?" she accused.

"Doesn't matter if I did or didn't. I'm here," he said.

"It matters to me, dammit," Aggie flung back.

"Guess you'll have to keep wondering," Fargo said, and turned to the door.

"I don't have to wonder," Aggie called after him, but he heard the quaver in her voice and he closed the door behind him without answering. He saw Zeke asleep in a corner and took down his own bedroll, laid out his still-wet clothes, and relaxed as the sound of rushing water filled the darkness. Aggie's angry, hurt words circled inside him. Her very personal wounds were not the only thing that brought her here. He believed that much. But he wondered if she'd be as driven without them. Alicia's determination was icy greed, Aggie's a bitter harvest. He wondered which was worse as he closed his eyes and drew sleep around himself.

6

When morning came, he woke with the rain starting to hit hard against his face. He dressed quickly and saw Zeke and Ned pulling up the mooring line. Ben Higgens held the sail until Ned took over, and Fargo watched the old captain's portly face seem drawn.

"You afraid?" Fargo asked, and Zeke nodded.

"This river's rising too fast," the captain said. "We won't make it past the worst of it for another three days. She won't wait that long to flood."

Fargo glanced up and saw Aggie there, a yellow rainslicker over her shirt and Levi's. "We're going on. If she floods, we'll have to ride it out," she said, and Fargo saw Joe Kreiser come up to stand beside her. "Help me feed the lambs," she said to the youth, and turned away.

Fargo waited till she was inside the cabin and mixing feed before he turned to Zeke. "Can we ride it out if she floods?" he asked.

"Not likely," Zeke said.

"Can we tie up and weather it?" Fargo queried.

"Not likely," Zeke repeated. "If we could find a spot, chances are the moorning lines would go."

"You saying there's nothing to do?" Fargo frowned.

"Aggie wants to go on," the old captain said. "Nothing's a hundred percent sure. Maybe she'll be lucky."

Fargo glanced over at Ben and the man shrugged helplessly. "I can't be leaving her," Ben said.

"Me neither," Zeke added. "Ned won't either."

Fargo straightened up and leaned against the rail as Aggie came from the cabin with Joe and began to feed the lambs. She kept the canvas over the corral to keep the rain out, and Fargo's eyes were cold steel as they swept the others. They were old and tired men, fatalists who had let a sense of loyalty replace the will to live. They didn't want to die. They just hadn't the strength to fight to live any longer. They were getting a strange sense of comfort and belonging in following Aggie. Her determination had enveloped all of them. She'd given them a purpose in life and they were giving her love and loyalty. And none of it changed the facts, Fargo swore silently. She'd die if the river flooded, she and all her plans and everyone else.

Fargo swore again. He'd come this far with her. He was damned if he'd let it all go down because of her hardheaded stubborn stupidity. He waited till she and Joe came out from beneath the canvas with the empty feed pails.

"I've coffee on," Aggie said as she walked to the cabin. "I'll have Joe bring it out to you."

The youth went into the cabin with her and emerged a few minutes later with a steaming mug of coffee, which he handed to Zeke. He brought two more out and gave one to Ned and another to Ben. He started to turn back to the cabin when Fargo passed him in three long strides.

"I'll get my own," he growled, and shut the door in the youth's face.

Aggie spun, frowned at him. "I said all I had to say last night," she told him.

"I didn't," Fargo said. "You've got to put in now, before it's too late."

"No," she answered.

"Those lambs are the heart of it. Without them you lose. You've got to put them ashore with the wagon," Fargo said.

"Oh, indeed, with Alicia and Ronan watching us. They'll be at us instantly," Aggie said.

"They can't cross the river that fast, not the way it is now. It's a better chance than staying on here," Fargo countered.

"It's giving her the lambs. Is this why you came back? To try to talk me into her hands? You're working for her, aren't you?" Aggie accused.

"I'm trying to save it all for you, including your stubborn ass," Fargo threw back.

"I can't trust you, not after you were with her. We're going on," Aggie insisted.

"Damn you, Aggie Baxter. You're alike, the two of you," Fargo roared.

"We are not," Aggie shouted hotly.

"You're as ruthless as she is. She's willing to sacrifice every damn man she's hired to win, and you're willing to sacrifice everyone on board to win. You're two sides to the same coin," Fargo blasted.

"That's not so, not so at all," Aggie screamed, her face darkened with fury. She strode to the door and yanked it open. "Get out. I don't want to hear anything else from you," she bit out.

"Damn fool girl," Fargo muttered as he walked from the cabin.

She came to the doorway. Joe Kreiser waited just outside. "Please see that Fargo doesn't come in my cabin again, Joe," she said icily.

"My pleasure," the youth said, and Fargo shook his head as he walked to the far side of the ark and sat down against the rail.

The wind had grown stronger and the rain came down with renewed force, but Fargo's eyes went to the river, where he saw pieces of branches and spray planking float by. Ned and Ben Higgens were hard-pressed to manage the sail together and Zeke strained at the tiller to keep the boat from being turned by the racing current. Joe had taken a post in front of the door and his young face held defiance and smugness. Fargo swore silently and watched the rushing river as thoughts raced through his mind with even faster speed.

Aggie was past reasoning with, he realized. Old wounds and new fears had turned determination into blind obsession. The bottom line throbbed out at him in his thoughts. He'd have to save her despite herself. He'd have to act. To do less would be to give Alicia her victory on a platter. Aggie couldn't win over the long haul. There was still too much stacked against her. He hadn't changed his mind on that. But she didn't deserve to lose by her own stupidity. He had to act, he grunted grimly and shut off thoughts and leaned back to wait.

The morning had ended when Aggie stepped from the cabin and scanned the racing waters. Her face was made of defiant confidence, and she ignored the pieces of trees and the debris that rushed past. If she noticed that the river was lapping high on its banks, she gave no sign of it. The angry purple-black sky remained in the distance as the ark made painfully slow progress into the swift current, and Aggie tossed an encouraging smile at Zeke as she returned to the cabin.

Kreiser stayed near the bow, Fargo saw, but his young eyes missed little that went on anywhere on the boat. When Aggie emerged again later in the afternoon, she called to the youth and he came at once, slipping on the wet deck along the starboard rail. "Can you cut some of the dried-beef strips into stewing pieces for me, Joe?" she asked sweetly, and Joe nodded eagerly and followed her into the cabin.

Fargo caught her quick glance at him as she closed the door and he saw the icy dismissal in it. He held his face expressionless and stayed by the rail until he felt the ark swerve toward shore. He saw Zeke holding the tiller to one side and then he glimpsed the point of land that jutted out into the river some hundred yards ahead. The rushing waters left a relatively untouched, calm spot back of the point. "We'll moor there for the night," Zeke said, though there was at least another hour till dark.

He watched Zeke and Ned bring the boat into the quieter pool of water and drop anchor before he rose to his feet and walked to where Ben had just lowered the sail. There were things he had to find out now, he reasoned. He addressed his first question to Zeke. "Can you bring her right up to the bank?" he asked.

"Reckon I could," Zeke said. "This high water will keep her from getting stuck. Why?"

"That's what I want you to do later tonight," he said. He saw the old captain's eyes question and he glanced at the other two men, saw their eyes on him. "I'm going to save her ass," he growled. "She's all wrong to try to go farther upriver, and you know it." Zeke shrugged and Fargo took the three in with one glance. "I'm asking you not to get in my way," he said.

He watched the three men exchange glances, and it was Ben Higgens who decided to speak for them. "We won't try to stop you," he murmured. "But we won't try to help you, either."

"Fair enough," Fargo said.

"The kid won't stay still for it," Zeke warned.

"I know that," Fargo said.

"He's trying to help her in his own way, too. Don't take him out," Ben said.

"I won't," Fargo said. "Unless I have to." He turned away and sat down by the rail again, stayed there as darkness fell.

Aggie came out with plates and a kettle of stew. Fargo let everyone else eat first and then took a plate for himself, and when he finished, he handed her the plate. "Get off the river," he murmured. "Use your head for something else besides wearing a bonnet."

"Go back to Alicia," she hissed, and strode away.

Fargo purposefully started to follow and the youth

111

stepped out to block his path, one hand on his gun butt. Skye halted, seemed to hesitate, and then turned away. But he saw the glint of disdain come into the youth's eyes, and he smiled inwardly. He wanted Joe to feel he'd only to threaten to win. Misplaced confidence was always an ally. He slumped down against the rail and listened to the mooring rope groan as the water tugged at the boat.

Joe made himself comfortable beside the cabin door and Fargo let the night move on, aware of Zeke's, Ben's and Ned's nervous glances at him and at one another. Finally, as Fargo made no move to do anything, the three men took their weather gear and blankets and bedded down for the night.

Fargo let himself sleep in spurts and each time he woke the water seemed to race faster around the point of land. But he continued to catnap until he woke again and sat up, dawn not more than an hour or so away, he estimated. Aggie would be wild with rage when he finished, and he wanted her to have the dawn light to come after him. Alicia and the others on the opposite shore wouldn't realize anything for at least an hour or two after dawn, and when they did, they'd be unable to cross the racing river for perhaps another two or three days.

His plans were far from foolproof, but they were the best he could do under the circumstances. Maybe not the best, he corrected himself, but the only damn thing possible. He pushed himself to his feet with no attempt at silence and saw Joe Kreiser's eyes snap open at once. The youth pushed out from under his blanket and got to his feet as Fargo started toward the cabin.

"Stay right there," the youth said.

"Want to talk to her," Fargo growled, and moved forward, his eyes narrowed on the youth.

Joe Kreiser yanked his six-gun out and leveled it at him, and Fargo stopped. "Get back," Joe said.

Fargo halted, paused in place for a moment, then shrugged and started to step backward. But he had seen what he wanted to see. Joe Kreiser's draw was only moderately fast and marred by a touch of nervousness. "Guess I can wait," Fargo muttered, and started to turn away. Out of the corner of his eye he saw Joe Kreiser drop his gun back into its holster, a glimmer of relief in his face. With the speed of a cougar's spin, Fargo turned, the Colt flying into his hand, and he saw Joe yank at his gun as surprise flooded his unlined face. Joe had the gun clear of its holster when Fargo fired, and the youth cursed as the gun flew from his hand, Fargo's shot slamming into the cylinder. The gun skittered across the deck, and with more bravery than sense, Joe dived after it. Fargo crossed the deck in two long strides and was beside the youth just as Joe closed his hand around the gun. Fargo brought the butt of the heavy Colt down on the back of Joe Kreiser's head and the youth went limp and lay facedown on the deck.

Zeke, Ben, and Ned were up, their eyes glued to the scene. Fargo kicked Joe's gun over to Ned. "Keep it for him," he muttered, and turned as the cabin door flew open. Aggie, clothed in the bare-shouldered nightgown, stared in alarm, and shock took over her face as she saw Joe on the deck with Fargo standing over him.

"Bastard," she breathed, spun, and darted back into the cabin.

Fargo dug his heels into the deck as he spurted forward and raced into the cabin. He caught her around the waist just as she tried to bring the rifle out of the corner; he yanked the gun out of her hands and flung it aside. He pulled away as she tried to claw at him and he felt her knee come up, twisted, and took the blow on the outside of his thigh.

"Goddamn you," Aggie swore as she twisted and fought with furious anger. He let go of her, ducked low

113

as she swung at him, and caught her around the legs, lifted, and tossed her onto the mattress on the floor. She landed with a yelp and he glimpsed firm-fleshed, sturdy legs before she rolled, tried to dive for the rifle again.

He caught her arm and yanked her back, picked up the small, furiously struggling form, and slammed it down hard on the mattress. He felt the breath go out of her and she lay still for a moment and gulped in air. It was enough time for him to pull down the clothes-line stretched inside the cabin and wrap it around her wrists. He tied the line to her ankles so she could do little more than bring her knees up together.

"Rotten bastard," Aggie hissed. "Traitor. Damn no-good, stinking traitor."

"Got your breath back, I see," Fargo said as he finished tying her securely.

Her bare shoulders twisted as she tried to free herself and one modest breast pushed upward almost out of the nightgown and she lay back to glare at him. "Damn you, Fargo. Damn her. May you both rot in hell," Aggie shouted.

"I haven't time to argue with you," Fargo said. "You wouldn't listen anyway." He strode from her and heard her turning and twisting in helpless fury atop the mattress. He closed the door behind him and halted beside the inert figure on the deck. Joe Kreiser would remain unconscious for a good while, but Fargo decided to take no chances and used a length of his lariat to tie the youth hand and foot. He turned to where Ben, Zeke, and Ned watched him with grave faces.

"Take her into shore," he said, and Zeke and Ben began to pull the mooring line up.

Fargo went to the big converted hay wagon and peered into the interior. A toolbox provided a long roll of stout twine and he motioned to Ben Higgens as he strode to the corral that held the lambs. "Put a rope collar on each one," he said, and Ben nodded. Fargo worked quickly, cutting, tying, and fashioning the small collars that were slipped onto each lamb, but it took time and he heard Aggie call out for help. "Ignore her," he growled.

When the rope collars were on each lamb, he had Ben help him run a rope lead from collar to collar so the little sheep were all tied to one another. "Now we put them into the wagon," he said, and opened the corral gate. Ned helped lift the sheep into the spacious interior of the wagon and Fargo saw that the ark had been steered almost to the high water against the riverbank. "Hitch the team up," he ordered, and saw Ben hesitate.

"Put your gun on me," the man said.

"Why?" Fargo frowned.

"It'll make me feel better about what I'm doing," Ben said.

Fargo nodded, understood, and obliged as he drew the Colt out and let the hammer click. Ben hurried to bring the horses to the wagon and Fargo turned to Zeke and Ned. "You can lower the boarding plank," he said, and both men nodded gravely.

Fargo tied the Ovaro to the back of the big Bucks County hay wagon and put four bags of feed for the lambs inside while Ben finished hitching the team. Done, Ben took one of the horses by the cheek strap and began to lead the team toward the boarding plank. Fargo climbed onto the driver's seat of the wagon, took the reins, and put the canvas over the bows of the main body of the wagon. He paused to look down at the three figures who watched him with grave, drawn faces. "You know I'm doing right. These lambs drown and she's finished, and you know they'll drown if the boat goes under." He shot a quick glance up at the sky and saw only inky blackness, but he knew the dawn was near. "Tell her you watched me go north," he said.

"Is that where you're going?" Ben asked.

"Yes, onto high ground and north," Fargo said. "I'll move slow, give you time to catch up. You've two horses left."

"Aggie will call the shots soon as we untie her," Ben said. "She'll figure you're on your way to meet with Alicia."

"And try to stop me before I do," Fargo said. "That's all I want." He snapped the reins as the ark swerved, and he steered the horses down the boarding plank. The boat was close enough to shore so that they touched bottom by the time the water reached their briskets and he felt the wagon lurch downward as it left the plank but quickly float behind the horses as they pulled for shore. He snapped the reins again and the wagon wheels touched bottom and rolled up onto the bank. He cast a glance back at the ark and saw the craft slide away from shore as the current caught at it. He sent the wagon forward and the land rose at once, and he let the horses move on their own through the brush and the trees beyond.

In the distance, he caught the first glimmer of the gray dawn. Aggie's rage would shatter when she found he hadn't brought the lambs to Alicia. She'd see what anger and stubbornness refused to let her see now, that she and the lambs were alive and not at the bottom of the Mississippi. He allowed himself a small smile of satisfaction as he drove through the still-inky dark.

As morning came, unrelieved grayness slid across the land, and the rain began again, heavier this time, an angry sound as it beat against the leaves. Fargo had found a moose trail wide enough for the wagon that ran in almost a straight line north. The wagon tracks would be easy to pick up in the rain-softened ground and he moved with deliberate slowness. It was mid-morning when he halted at a spot where the trail widened into a half-circle before narrowing where it led on farther. He drew the wagon under a very wide-spreading box-elder and climbed into the back. The lambs had enough room to move about although they were tied to one another, but they preferred to huddle close together. He lay down against one side of the long wagon and let himself rest.

He lay still and listened for the sound of hoofbeats or footsteps, but the only thing he heard was the steady beat of the rain against the canvas and the creak of the wagon as an occasional hard gust of wind swept through the hillside. The morning wore on and he felt the frown of uneasiness dig into his brow as he sat up and climbed back onto the driver's seat. The morning was drawing close to noon, he knew, even without a sun to help pinpoint time. They should have caught up with him by now, even on foot, and they had two horses to use. He peered down the rainswept moose trail, searched for a sign of approching figures, and saw only the wet emptiness. The uneasiness that had stabbed at him now curled into a knot inside his stomach. He took up the reins and moved the wagon deep back beyond the box elder until it was hidden from sight. He checked the lambs again—they were restless but contained—and he swung down from the wagon, unhitched the Ovaro, and sent the horse back down the trail the way he had come.

As he rode, his gaze searched the trail ahead, hoping to see pursuing riders appear, and he turned downhill when the trail came to an end. When the slope began to level off, he saw the tracks of the wagon wheels where he'd rolled up from the bank. He slowed, expected to see the ark when he pushed through the trees, and felt his jaw drop as he looked out at nothing but the racing river.

"Damn," he swore aloud. She hadn't left the ark to pursue him. "Damn her," he swore again, wheeled the pinto around, and raced north. The water was higher than he'd ever seen it, the riverbank no longer visible, and he rode through the trees.

He wanted to believe Zeke had convinced Aggie to turn back and run before the rushing waters, but he knew better. She'd never agree to that. Instead of going ashore after him, she'd gone upriver. She figured to sail past him, then put in, double back on shore, and take him by surprise from the north. Stupid, damn hardhead, he swore as he raced forward. He held the pinto at a fast canter as he wove through the trees that were now all but touching the water. He'd gone on perhaps a half-mile, his eyes peering out at the river to find the ark, when he heard the sound. A hissing roar first, it came from upriver, grew stronger, and seemed to fill the air and then the very world. He slowed the Ovaro and stared upriver as the sound enveloped him, and then he saw it: a tremendous wall of water coming downriver. It curled foam-white at the crest, sweeping everything before it, trying to spread out on both sides as if it wanted to devour the land. As he yanked the Ovaro in a tight circle and sent the horse uphill, he spotted the ark, turning as if in a giant whirlpool.

The boat rode high on the crest of towering water, vanished from sight for a moment as the crest rolled on beyond it, and came up into view again, still turning as the floodwaters spun it in a tight circle. He reined up beside a sandbar willow and saw the small figures clinging to the boat, and as he watched, the crest of the roaring floodwaters caught the ark again. The craft seemed to skid across the top of the water toward the shore and he saw one end of the cabin had collapsed but the two horses were still aboard, still tied to the stern post. As the spinning boat came nearer, he made out Zeke's portly form clinging to the useless tiller and he could see Ned stretched out on the deck. The ark spun again as the rushing floodwaters lifted it high and sent a cascade of spray over it, and he could see little else. He heard his voice shouting curses and knew the feeling of complete helplessness. Suddenly, as the racing floodwaters surged in powerful riptides, the ark was lifted again, spun around the other way, and sent toward him with breathtaking speed on the power of a surging crosscurrent. This time he glimpsed the close-cropped hair and the small form clinging to the cabin door, which lay half off its hinges.

It would soon upend, he knew. It would be but a matter of minutes. The boat continued to rush toward him as it turned first one way, then the other. He leapt from the Ovaro, pulled a length of extra lariat from his saddlebag, and tied one end around the tree trunk. With the other end in hand, he stepped to the very edge of the water that leapt along the trees. The ark was below where he waited and its pass close enough, he saw as he readied the lariat. The river took the craft again, sent it swerving to one side as it came almost abreast of him. Fargo heard the whistle as the rope whirled through the rain and saw it land over the bow cleat. It snapped taut, held for a moment, and then broke with the sound of his Sharps being fired.

"Goddamn," Fargo swore as the boat swept past. He spun and vaulted onto the Ovaro as he saw the ark begin to lift at the stern. The rushing waters caught it, sent it into the air as though it were a child's toy boat. Fargo glimpsed the figures flung into the rushing waters as the craft poised on end, but he had his now-shortened lariat out and whirling. He sent it whistling throught the air with all the skill he possessed and saw it close around a flailing arm. He tightened, pulled, and saw Ned's long form come out of the water and onto the bank. Fargo wrapped the other end of the lariat around a low branch and held Ned safely on the bank as he sent the Ovaro into a gallop. Peering into the river, he spotted the close-cropped hair being turned over by the rushing river. The crest of the roaring floodwaters had passed but the terrible current surged with a furious power of its own.

Aggie vainly tried to swim, but he saw it was impossible as she was simply spun and buffeted. He sent the Ovaro racing downriver past Aggie's twisting form. The only chance was to get below her, he knew, and when he was past her enough, he sent the Ovaro into the river. He felt the power of the current clutch at the horse at once, but the pinto put all the drive of his powerful hindquarters into swimming. Aggie was sweeping down toward him and he saw her go under, fight back up again. But she couldn't last much longer, and he cursed as he saw her near. She was too far out and he slammed his hand down hard on the horse's rump. The horse swam forward an extra thrust, fighting the current, which tried to sweep him aside, but Fargo felt the powerful legs tiring. Aggie was near, but still too far away, and Fargo yanked the horse around and let the current sweep him downriver at an angle. Aggie's form came up behind him, drew closer, and he swerved the Ovaro once more as she swept by.

He stretched forward, more out of the saddle than in, managed to close a hand around her arm and pull her toward him. She came, her body limp, her eyes closed, and he cursed into the river and the rain. As he pulled her across the saddle on her stomach, he saw the ark rise up again and overturn completely this time. The rope holding the horses gave way and he saw the two animals plunge into the water and furiously strike out for shore as the current swept them downriver. He let the Ovaro move toward shore at an angle, pushed by the river, and he heard Aggie retching, the sound suddenly wonderfully sweet. She was still throwing up riverwater when the Ovaro touched bottom and began to pull up onto the land. Fargo spurred the horse onto dry ground and halted.

Aggie slid from the saddle and he caught her and

lowered her gently to the ground. She lay coughing, chest heaving, half on her stomach.

"Don't move," he said. "Stay there and don't move." He rose and took the pinto down along the rushing river. He saw the ark, on its back, moving slowly now. The horses had found their way to shore somewhere, he was certain, and he rode slowly, squinting along the edge of the water. He finally spotted the two figures, lying perhaps a dozen yards apart, both crumpled onto dry ground. He sent the pinto forward, leapt down when he reached the first figure, and saw Zeke's portly shape. The other was Ben Higgens, he saw. Zeke was alive, gasping in air, shock and pain on his round face.

Fargo moved on to kneel beside Ben Higgens and the man opened his eyes as he coughed up water and a little blood. "I have Aggie," he said. "I'm north, up from the river. Come along when you can."

Ben blinked agreement with his eyelids, and Fargo rose, returned to the Ovaro, and hurried back to where he'd left Aggie.

She had pushed herself up to a sitting position, he saw, and he halted, dismounted, and sank down on one knee beside her. She stared at him with eyes that wore only shock and horror. "The lambs are safe," he said. "Waiting for you."

Her eyes closed and she let her forehead fall against her arm. "Good God," she breathed. "Oh, God almighty." She opened her eyes slowly and pulled back to stare numbly at him. "I thought you were—" she began, and he broke in.

"Bringing them to Alicia," he finished. She nodded and looked away. "I got hold of Ned. Lady Luck was swimming with Ben and Zeke," Fargo said. "Don't know about anyone else."

"Joe's gone," Aggie said in a whispered monotone. "He was hit by a plank when the cabin gave way. It knocked him into the river unconscious." She halted, pressed both hands to her face. "My fault, all of it. I said we could make it upriver. My fault," she half-sobbed. He remained silent and she took her hands from her face to look at him.

"You want comfort?" Fargo said tightly. "Words to ease your conscience?"

"Maybe. Something to help. I didn't do it on purpose," Aggie said.

"You've come to the wrong place," Fargo said coldly.

"You have to be cruel?"

"Stupidity's cruel. Not caring about anything but yourself is cruel," he threw back at her, and she looked away and pressed her face into her hands again.

"Yes," she said, her voice small and muffled. "Yes."

"I'll be back," Fargo said, and rose to his feet. He left the Ovaro beside her to rest and began to walk north. He'd gone around the bend, perhaps a few hundred yards, when he saw the tall, thin figure come toward him. Ned's face seemed almost cadaverous as he came up, and he was still taking deep breaths, Fargo saw.

"I owe you, friend. I won't ever be able to pay you back, but I owe you," Ned breathed.

"I was there at the right time," Fargo said. "Zeke made it somehow. Ben Higgens, too."

"Aggie?" Ned asked, his eyes wide. Fargo nodded and Ned lifted his long face skyward. "Merciful God," he intoned. He fell into step beside Fargo, and the Trailsman walked slowly while Ned struggled to gather his strength back. When they rounded the bend, they saw the two figures beside Aggie. Zeke and Ben peered at Fargo with gratitude pushing through the exhaustion in their faces.

"We damn near paid for it, didn't we?" Ben Higgens said.

"Paid for what?" Fargo frowned.

"Not having the guts to say no," the older man said. "For being weak."

"Loyalty's not being weak," Fargo said. "Caring

too much isn't being weak. But it can be wrong. I'll go bring the wagon back.

"No, we'll walk," Zeke said.

"It's a fair haul," Fargo warned.

"For us it'll be a celebration," Ben said, and Fargo smiled and understood. He paused beside Aggie with the Ovaro.

"You can ride with me," he offered.

"No, thank you. I'll walk with the others," she said gravely, and he nodded, climbed onto the horse, and began to lead the way. Her refusal was a form of apology to Ben and the others and a kind of self-punishment, he realized. He'd not try to change it. She deserved whatever she gave herself, he grunted bitterly.

He rode the horse at a walk along the moose trail when he reached it, and while Ben, Zeke, and Ned exchanged passing remarks, Aggie stayed silent, walked with her eyes almost downcast. Only when they reached the wagon did she explode in a burst of glee as she climbed inside with the lambs. When she came out, the rain had stopped and a warm sun pushed through the last of low-flying clouds.

Fargo took off wet clothes down to his trousers and Ned, Zeke and Ben, did the same.

"I've clothes in a trunk in the wagon," Aggie said. "Give me a minute?"

Fargo nodded, and when she came out again, she wore fresh Levi's and a dark-red shirt. She hung her wet clothes on the tail of the wagon and Zeke grunted his words. "We've got to get us some more duds someplace," he said. "Can't spend a winter with one set of clothes."

"I'll find us a town, I hope," Fargo said. "Before we head too far inland."

"Got any idea where we are?" Ben asked.

"Minnesota," Fargo said. "This is Minnesota land." He pointed into the distance where the blue of a large lake glistened under the sun. "Land of lakes, all sizes and shapes."

"Is that what the name means?" Aggie asked.

"In a way. A proper translation of the Indian name is 'the Place Where the Sky Is in the Land,' " Fargo explained.

"Because of all the sky-blue lakes," Aggie followed, and Fargo nodded. "Well, we came to find a place to settle in. Let's do it," she said.

"What about Alicia?" Ben Higgens asked.

"Forget Alicia," Aggie replied. "That's one good thing that's come out of all that happened. She had to see the overturned ark. She'll figure we're all gone. She's probably on her way back now."

"Maybe," Fargo grunted.

"Why maybe?" Aggie frowned.

"Seeing the ark may not satisfy her. She's taken no chances up to now. She might decide to look further," Fargo said.

"That doesn't mean she'll pick up our trail," Aggie said. "The river's still running too fast to cross. Then, if they decide to search, they have to search the other side too."

"True enough," Fargo agreed. "But she hasn't missed a trick this far. Don't count on her to start now."

"She's given up," Aggie said confidently. "Let's get on with what we came here to do."

The sudden noise of brush being trampled broke off further talk. "Under the wagon," Fargo yelled as he drew the Colt and ducked behind a tree. He was crouched, the gun aimed, when the brush parted and a brown mare with a black mane came out from the trees, riderless and saddleless.

"She's from the ark," Ned called out, and crawled from beneath the wagon. The brown mare pawed the ground and seemed happy to see them. She had a piece of rope still around her neck and Ned took hold of it and led her forward. She came at once.

"There's an extra bridle in the tailbox of the wagon," Aggie said, and Ben hurried to fetch it.

"Maybe the other one's around," Ben said. "We'll go have a look." He strode into the forest with Zeke at his heels and Aggie helped Ned put the extra bridle on the mare. He returned a few minutes later. "No sign of the other," he said.

"One's better than none, even without a saddle," Fargo said.

"I can ride bareback," Aggie put in, and rummaged in the wagon again to emerge with a blanket she lay across the horse's back in Indian fashion.

Fargo watched her pull herself on the mare with a quick, graceful motion, settle her firm, round rear down on the blanket. Ben took the reins on the wagon and Zeke and Ned climbed on beside him. Fargo brought the Ovaro up front and led the way up the hillside to where the land leveled off in a long plateau fashioned of mostly flat ground and good forest stands. With enough of the day left to make time, he led on, spurred the pinto forward, and left the others behind. He searched the land as he rode, his eyes narrowed, and when he returned, he took the others to a brook that crossed a trail around a long stand of ironwood that was already shedding its seed bags.

Aggie fed the lambs as the horses took in water and Ben filled the water keg on the wagon. When Aggie finished, she came up to the small hillock where Fargo stood, his lake-blue eyes narrowed as he scanned the land. "Looking for Alicia?" she said with a hint of disdain in her voice.

"No," Fargo said.

"Then you've decided I'm right?" Aggie asked.

"No," he said, and she frowned back. "I'm looking for Indian," Fargo said. "Ojibwa and Santee Dakota. Saw plenty of signs along the way."

"Are they dangerous?" Aggie asked.

"Dangerous enough. Maybe not like the Cheyenne

or the Sioux or the Assiniboin, but they're Indians and all that lamb's wool would make nice winter caps," Fargo said. He turned and she walked back to the wagon with him in silence.

"Follow the edge of the ironwoods," he told Ben. "I'm going ahead and try to get us supper."

Ben nodded and Fargo put the Ovaro into a trot and moved on, hugged the tree line, and finally spotted a pair of large cottontails. He drew the Sharps from its saddle case, halted the Ovaro, and took aim. He fired, two shots so fast they sounded almost as one, and both rabbits lay still. Aggie and the wagon came up soon, and Ben started for the rabbits.

"I'll have them skinned and ready for the pot by the time we stop for the night," Ben said, and gave the reins to Zeke.

Fargo rode on quickly, put the pinto into a fast canter, and left the others behind. He spied more unshod pony tracks before the day drew to a close, all small parties, he noted, most likely hunting deer. He found a place where the trees moved back in a half-circle as dusk began to settle down, and he waved the wagon in as he swung to the ground. Aggie took an iron stewpot from the tailbox, gathered small firewood, and had the rabbits stewing before night descended.

Fargo stretched out, dozed, and woke when the meal was ready. He felt the coolness of the night wind as he ate, and he sat back when he finished, a grimness holding his chiseled countenance.

Aggie peered appraisingly at him when she collected his empty tin plate. "You're thinking something and it's not making you happy," she remarked.

"Bull's-eye," he said, and she waited questioningly. "You too thick-skinned to feel that wind?" he tossed at her.

"I feel it," Aggie said.

"It's talking wind, telling you that winter's not far off," he said.

"You still don't think I can pull it off," she said.

"You haven't enough time left to build a proper place and stock it to last through a Minnesota winter," Fargo said.

"You find us a spot and we'll do it," Aggie said, and strode away.

All the hardheaded determination had returned, he saw, and now perhaps it was for the best. She'd need every bit of it to have any kind of chance. He took his bedroll, paused to peer across the flatland under a half-moon, and moved into the trees. He settled down a dozen or more yards from the wagon, undressed, and put the Colt alongside the bedroll where he could reach it instantly. He slid into his bedroll, relaxed, and let the questions that still waited fade away. He had slowly begun to doze when his ears caught the sound of underbrush being rustled. His hand closed around the Colt as he pushed up on one elbow. His eyes were focused on the bushes when he saw the small form step out and move toward him.

He sat up, pushed the Colt back into the holster, and watched her halt before him. "What the hell are you doing roaming through the brush?" he growled.

"Couldn't sleep. I keep thinking about young Joe," she said, and lowered herself to the ground beside him. She wore the very loose, billowy nightdress that made her look lost inside it.

"That won't do him or you any good now," Fargo said coldly.

"Ben and Zeke and Ned are trying to be so kind to me it makes me feel worse."

"You know that won't be my way. That why you came here?"

"Maybe, in a way, but there's more, things I have to say," she answered gravely.

"Go on," Fargo said, and saw her glance move across the muscled nakedness of his torso.

"I'll make it, but it'll be because of what you did. I want you to know that I know that, Fargo," she said. "Maybe it's a little thing, but I keep thinking that you came back and it's not a little thing to me. You're the only man who's ever come back to me after Alicia got her hands on him."

"Guess I'm just different," Fargo said.

"And I was so wrong. You kept asking me what I was afraid of and you know now what it was. But Alicia was wrong too," Aggie said.

"How?" Fargo questioned.

"She said money was all you'd ever get from me," Aggie answered, and using both hands with an explosion of quick motion, she yanked the loose nightdress over her head and flung it on the grass.

Fargo's eyes took in the very modest breasts, almost small yet very beautifully rounded, fitting her slender body to perfection, tiny pink tips on equally tiny pink circles, breasts as pert and saucy as she was. Beneath their rounded loveliness, a flat abdomen narrowed to a small waist, and his gaze moved down to where a slightly convex curve offered a provocative little belly that went down into a very neat dark triangle, so small and so neat it almost seemed clipped. Legs that were somehow both slender and rounded were held tightly together, and Fargo finally brought his gaze back to her eyes.

"You just want to prove her wrong?" Fargo asked.

"No, and this isn't trying to say thanks. I'm here because I want to be here, and it's damn cold out here."

Fargo lifted the bedroll cover and she half-rose, swung on her firm, round rear, and pushed herself into the bedroll beside him. "Oh, gosh." She shivered and pressed against the warmth of his body. Her breasts were very firm, the tiny pink tips pushing into him, and her arms went around his neck. "Oh, migosh," Aggie whispered. "It feels so good. You feel so good."

Fargo moved, turned her onto her back, and she lay still as he enjoyed the small, firm beauty that was hers, everything proportioned, balanced, every line and curve of her neat and pert. She clearly was flesh echoing spirit, and when his lips pressed her mouth open, she waited, hardly responded until his tongue passed lightly into her, touched her lips, circled, caressed, and her mouth opened, welcomed, breathed delight.

His hand moved slowly down over her breastbone, caressed skin, and he felt her quiver. When his hand closed around one modest breast, she cried out in a spasm of utter delight and her arms tightened around his neck. "My gosh, oh, oh," Aggie breathed and her cry became a mixture of panic and protest as his hand moved down across the flat abdomen, halted on the rounded belly, and came to rest on the neat nap. "No," she gasped out. "Oh, no, oh, ohmigosh." He held his hand atop the clipped-like mound, pressed his thumb through the short, dense fuzz. Her legs came up pressed tight together, bent left and right, from side to side as one, and he brought his mouth down to the very modest breasts. He drew one in, pulled gently on the tiny pink tip.

"Aaaaah . . . oh, oh, gosh, oh, gosh," Aggie cried, and kept her legs together as they twisted from side to side. Fargo rose up, brought his torso over her, and the hot, pulsating organ pressed into the neat nap. "Aaaaiiii . . . oh, oh, oh," Aggie murmured, and he pressed down harder, pushed the erect hotness of him into the tight space between her legs, let it lift upward to touch the tip of her moist orifice.

Aggie screamed, thrill mixed with fear, wanting combined with apprhension, but he stayed, let his pulsating flesh hold against her, and slowly her thighs began to part, trembling as they did. He pressed deeper, brought himself up tight against the moist edge of the clipped nap, and Aggie made a sharp, gasped noise. Her hips lifted and her thighs fell apart as a flower suddenly coming open. "Oh, please, yes, oh, gosh, please," Aggie murmured, her voice little more than a whispered sound. He lifted again, slid forward into her dark warmth, and felt the tightness of her envelop him at once.

Aggie screamed, a sound unlike any she had ever made before or ever would again, an explosion of discovered ecstasy, and he slid further and the scream broke off into tiny, gasped cries. He drew back and felt her fingers dig into him in panic, relaxing as he came forward again and slid deep into her warm, wet tightness.

Aggie clung to him with her thighs as she pushed upward, welcomed him now, reveled in his throbbing flesh, which aroused, thrilled, opened new wonders of feeling, and she cried out in tiny gasped sounds until he began to thrust harder, faster, suddenly ramming through her warmth. Aggie pushed against him, every part of her clinging—arms, legs, hands, the firm breasts pressed hard into his chest—as though she tried to absorb him from outside as well as inside, flesh fused to flesh, sensation welded to sensation.

"Fargo," he heard her whisper suddenly, an urgency in her voice. "Fargo," she whispered again as though calling for his attention. "I . . . I . . . oh, ohmigosh, oh, oh," Aggie gasped, and he felt her curved belly draw in, almost leap forward, and her slender thighs curled around him, tightening as her legs straightened and grew rigid. The scream escaped her in a spiral of sound and he felt her tiny quaking vibrations, the current of rapture, and her strong, young back arched under him. "Oh, yes, yes, ohmighosh, oh, oh yes," she sputtered as the world became something it had never been before and would never quite be again.

She held rigid, softly quaking, for a surprisingly long moment, and when his pulsating wanting exploded inside her, she groaned in absolute and total pleasure. Finally, he felt the slender legs relax, fall away almost as a flower shedding its petals, but she clung to him softly, brought his face down to the smallish breasts, and sighed with the pleasure of touch. He stayed with her and she brought her legs up to curl around his hard-muscled abdomen, turned to lie almost on top of him.

He kissed her gently and she nuzzled against his chest. "They were sure wrong," Fargo said, and she brought her head up at once.

"Who?" She frowned.

"Those boys who passed you by for Alicia." Fargo smiled.

Her smile was quietly smug. "You didn't, and that's all that counts now," she murmured. "Can I stay here with you?"

"Why not?" he answered. "You said it was cold out there."

She gave a contented sigh, snuggled her small self hard against him, and was asleep in minutes.

He went to sleep soon and the chill night breeze blew across the bedroll. He wanted to share her confidence and her hope, but he realized it was impossible. The best he could do was hold her close.

7

She wanted to ride with him when morning came and
he'd no reason not to let her. Just as he'd had no
reason not to let her make love to him again when she
woke with the first rays of dawn. She'd brought her
slender but firm little body hard against him and her
legs had moved up and down across his groin, rub-
bing, touching, arousing her own desires as well as his.
She'd cried out in pure joy when he took each tiny
pink nipple into his mouth and caressed each with his
tongue, and this time her eagerness matched her wanting. The new sun had just peered across the horizon
when her scream drifted skyward, hung in the air, and
slowly vanished.

She'd fed the lambs before she rode from camp with
him, and he'd told Ben to take the wagon along the
tree line toward a distant rise. Aggie rode close beside, her firm breasts hardly bouncing as he put the
pinto into a canter and reached the top of the low rise.
Below, a mesalike expanse of flatland stretched and
he felt his breath draw in at the magnificence of the
sight that unfolded before him. Herds of wild horses
all but covered the land, some in knots of ten, others
in clusters of thirty and forty. Some were mustangs,
interbred Indian pony stock, some traces of cavalry
mounts that had gotten away, but a surprising number
of horses with unmistakable Arab blood.

"They're beautiful, all of them," Aggie breathed.

"Many of them were direct descendants of the horses the old *conquistadors* brought with them," Fargo said.

"How do you know?" She frowned.

"Its there, in their lines, the Arab blood in them. Coronado, Cortés, and De Soto all brought the Spanish barb with them. That's a variety of the Arab bred by the Moors in North Africa. You can still see it in their lines, their heads with that bulge on the forehead. The Arabs called it the *jibbah*," Fargo explained. "And they're all plenty fierce and plenty wild, I can promise you that." He took his eyes from the wild horses to scan the low plateau. The flatland held some tree cover, mostly short, twisted buckeye interspersed with rock formations that jutted up in clusters. But the land dipped at the far end, he saw. The buckeye grew thicker and less twisted and he saw what seemed to be passages that led downward. He spurred the Ovaro forward in a fast canter and Aggie hurried after him.

Some of the mustangs scattered as he rode across the mesalike plain. Others merely moved backward, and some, the larger herds made up mostly of the Arabian stock, stayed motionless in bold defiance. Fargo steered clear of the larger clusters, well aware of the wild power with which they could explode, and he edged his way along the side of the plain until he reached the far end. A wide passage between the tall buckeye appeared, became rimmed with alder, and he rode through it and slowed where two tall rock formations narrowed the passage as they rose up on both sides. Hardy mountain brush and a dozen scraggly elms grew out from between the rocks. He sent the Ovaro forward in a walk, Aggie beside him, and halted as the narrow passage opened up onto a long, low dip of land, too wide to be a true ravine but close enough to one. Not more than a hundred yards from the bottom of the passage a tumbledown shack and two adjoining structures sat silently in the center of the land.

He hurried the Ovaro down the narrow passage and reined up in front of the shack. It was larger than it had seemed from above, obviously had once been a livable cabin. Part of the rear roof was missing now.

Aggie dismounted as he did, walked beside him as he took in the two adjoining structures. One had been a barn of sorts, an ox yoke still on one wall; the other, with thicker walls, was in better condition, and he saw bins dividing the interior to mark it as having been a storehouse.

"It hasn't been lived in for years," Aggie remarked as she stepped into the main shack with him and small clouds of dust rose up underfoot. But there was a table, a stairway to a small loft at one end and the frame for a mattress still on the floor of the loft. "But somebody lived here once," Aggie said, and he heard the excitement come into her voice. "And somebody's going to live here again," she said. He let his lips purse in thought and she came to him, pressed her hands against his arm. "It's perfect. We won't have to build from scratch. We've time to fix it up before the winter sets in. We'll clean it and repair it and have it tight and snug in no time. It has a place for the lambs and a storehouse ready for use as soon as it's cleaned. God, it's just what we need, Fargo."

He nodded, her excitement catching. The place was unquestionably abandoned and long unused, and he walked outside again.

She followed with quick steps. "What are you thinking?" she asked as his eyes took in the outside of the place.

"I'm wondering why they left," he said.

"Maybe they weren't able to make a go of it," Aggie said. "Maybe their livestock died on them. Maybe they died. Maybe a whole lot of things. I really don't care. I know it's perfect for what I need now." She gestured to the grass that stretched on beyond the house from side to side of the wide ravine. "Sheep can graze here beautifully. Especially my Orkneys," she said. "And in time, I can build a bigger, better place somewhere else if I want to. Right now, this is made to order. With a little work," she added quickly.

Fargo walked into the main cabin again, his gaze scanning the walls and the floors as he pushed dust away with his boot. He strolled to the table, found two sturdy wooden chairs upended in one corner, and picked each up, examined it carefully. He was clearing a large area of dust away on the floor when Aggie came in.

"What are you trying to find?" she asked.

"Old bloodstains," he said, and she frowned. "I'm wondering if the Dakota did in whoever used to live here," he said.

She thought for a moment. "I don't care," she said. "If that's what happened, it was a long time ago. Chances are they wouldn't come back looking again."

"Probably not," he agreed.

"I'm not superstitious," Aggie said. "Whatever happened, it was long ago and this is now. I found a well outside, the bucket next to it. I put it down and drew up good water. This is where I'm going to stay."

Fargo scanned the shack again, stepped outside, and surveyed the adjoining barn and storage place. "Maybe you have lucked out after all," he said. "You go bring in Ben and the wagon. I'm going to look around some more."

She nodded, pulled herself onto the brown mare, and Fargo took the Ovaro north down the other end of the wide ravine. The grass grew heavier, softer, as he neared the far end, and he saw the land rise sharply in rocky walls that sealed the back end of the land. The land was something between a ravine and a valley, he decided, but the only way in was through the narrow passage they had entered. He turned the fact in his mind as he rode back and saw Aggie leading the wagon down the rock-bordered passage into the ravine.

Ben, Zeke, and Ned were out of the wagon and examining the place when Fargo rode up, the three men as delighted with what they found as Aggie had been.

"We can fix it up," Ben said. "There's enough timber up on the plateau and around the edges down here. We'll have to cut and haul, but we can do it."

Aggie turned to Fargo. "What'd you find down at the other end?" she asked.

"Good land. But this is the only way in," he told her.

"Nothing wrong with that, is there?" she said.

"It's good and bad," he said. "You're close enough so you can see anything coming in, but when the heavy snows come, that passage will be closed tight. You won't be getting out till a thaw comes."

"That doesn't bother me, not for the first year," she said. "I won't be driving any sheep yet and certainly not in winter."

"You'd best store up enough food. If you can't get out, chances are deer can't get in, so you won't be shooting any fresh game to tide you over." Fargo warned.

"We'll store up good, and I'm sure we can get out enough to get some fresh meat sometime," Ben put in.

"There's a good chance you can," Fargo agreed.

"Let's start housecleaning," Aggie said happily, and paused beside Fargo. "Will you stay on some to help?" she asked, her voice suddenly a low murmur.

"Just to help?"

"No, not just to help," she answered, her eyes glistening.

"In that case I might." He grinned and she hurried to the wagon. He let his gaze travel across the sides of the wide ravine, slowly taking in the steep slope and trees. A single intruder could find his way down but no band of horsemen could manage it, white or red. He brought the Ovaro to the side of what had been the small barn and heard Aggie's cry of delight as she uncovered splint brooms and shovels while Zeke brought other tools from inside the long box slung under the wagon. Fargo joined them, and by the time the afternoon began to draw to a close they had cleared the main house of dust and cobwebs and he had brought the stale surface water from the well so they could draw on fresh, clean water. Aggie brought her stewpot in and used it over the fireplace for a supper of beans and jerky.

As dusk deepened, Fargo saw deer come down the narrow passage into the ravine. "You'll have fresh meat tomorrow," he murmured to Ben. More than deer moved into the ravine, he noted when night fell and he heard raccoon, marten, bobcat, and possum. The sound of hoofbeats echoed down from the plateau above in sudden bursts as the great herds raced back and forth, but he saw none of the mustangs enter the ravine.

"Why not?" Aggie asked when he pointed the fact out to her.

"Because we're here. They're very careful. They come in. I saw plenty of hoofprints. But they'll stay out till they get used to us being here," he said.

"I told Ben, Zeke, and Ned they could sleep in the shack, now that we've got it cleaned up," she said.

"Where do you figure to sleep?" Fargo asked blandly.

"Three guesses," she said as she took his bedroll down from the Ovaro. "I'll use the loft when we get it fixed," she said. But I'm in no hurry," she added as she walked off with the bedroll. He followed her and she put the gear down a dozen yards from the house, pulled off clothes with haste, and all but leapt into the bedroll as the night wind came. Her eyes were on him as he undressed slowly, devouring, waiting, and he took his time with the smile held inside him.

"Hurry up, dammit," she called out finally. He laughed, pulled off the last piece of clothing and knew he had already begun to rise in anticipation. "Oh, gosh, oh, oh," Aggie gasped as he came in beside her, pressed himself against her, and she seemed to explode with fire and wanting, hunger and desire, and her small, firm body swarmed atop him, pressed, clung, cried out at the touch of flesh on flesh, and the moon had crossed high in the blue velvet sky when her last scream of pure pleasure curled across the ravine.

She lay beside him, the small breasts lifting high as she took in deep drafts of air and slowly relaxed. Lifting on one elbow, the tiny pink tips twin pressure points against his chest, she let a smile of smug triumph touch her lips. "Still think I'm not going to make a go of it?" she asked almost teasingly.

He let himself think for a moment. "You've a better start than I expected you would have," he said. "But that won't make it go all by itself. Luck's got to stay with you."

"It will," she said. "You know you're a terrible pessimist, Fargo."

He nodded and kept the frown inside himself. It was more than pessimism, he knew, an inner apprehension that refused to fade away. He closed his eyes and held her to him as he uttered a silent prayer his misgivings proved wrong. Sometimes it was good to be wrong. He hoped this was one of those times.

The night drew into morning in stillness and he woke with the day, kissed the small form beside him, and she clung for an extra minute before pulling on clothes.

Later, after coffee, it was Ben who came to him while he cleared the old boards from the broken section of the roof. "We could do it for sure if you'd stay on, Fargo," the older man said.

"I can't," Fargo said. "I've my own trails to follow."

"Just thought I'd ask. You've done enough, I know," Ben said. "Has Aggie asked you to stay on?"

"In her own way," Fargo said. "I'll do this much. I'll stay till the first snow."

"Fair enough," the older man said happily.

"I'm going to ride out this morning, see if I can find a town someplace," Fargo said. "Could be a day, maybe two before I find one. I figure there has to be something not much farther than that. I'll bring you all a change of clothes back."

"And some extra work clothes if you can," Zeke's voice chimed in, and Fargo nodded as he went to the Ovaro and saddled the horse.

Aggie appeared, her face grave. "Hear you're going to find a town. Be careful," she said. "If they've a dress or a skirt, you could bring them to me. Small, if you can. Any size if not. I'll take 'em in."

"Be back as soon as I can," he said.

She leaned against him. "You know I'll be waiting," she said, and he ran his hand through the short-cropped brown hair before he swung into the saddle. He put the horse into a canter as he rode up through the passageway and onto the high plateau. The wild horses still stretched across the land and he saw every head go up as he started across the thick, rich grama grass. He had gone halfway across the plateau when the line of horses appeared in his path. But these had riders, one with flowing black hair that glistened in the sun. Ronan's large frame sat astride the horse close to Alicia's side, and the man bent low in the saddle. He was picking up the wagon tracks and they'd lead him right to the passage into the ravine, Fargo swore silently. But maybe they could be drawn off, he decided. It was worth a try.

He sent the Ovaro into a trot, changed to a canter, and went into a full gallop. He saw Alicia and the others wheel their mounts at once as they saw him racing for the far end of the plains where the forest of alders and red cedar spread a thick curtain of green.

They came after him and he angled the Ovaro for the trees, glanced back, and made a fast count that told him they had the same twenty riders they had before. He reached the trees and plunged into the woods, Alicia and her band only minutes behind. He swerved the pinto back and forth, let the horse crash through the underbrush with noisy abandon until the sound of his flight filled the forest and made it impossible for them to focus in on him. He circled, doubled back, swerved forward and sideways, and saw the pursuing riders stream into the woods. He heard muffled orders shouted and watched the men break up into small units to scour the forest. He slid from the Ovaro, walked the horse carefully behind thick foliage, and watched the men move through the woods in pairs, scattering in all directions.

He circled outside the area where they searched, carefully doubled back, and halted as he saw the white shirt and black hair moving alone. Alicia was staying behind while her men searched, and he left the Ovaro behind a thick cedar and moved forward in a crouch, the Colt in his hand.

He came up alongside her in the brush and saw her sit her mount with cool confidence. Once again, he was struck by how different she was from Aggie, flesh echoing spirit, he mused. But he took a moment to enjoy the cool beauty of her, long legs relaxed, breasts a long, lovely curve upward. It was a moment of indulgence and he paid the price for it as he heard the voice rasp from the brush half behind him. "Don't move or you're a dead man, Fargo," Ronan said.

Fargo stayed motionless and saw Alicia whirl in the saddle to peer toward him. "You shoot and she's a dead woman," Fargo said quietly, not turning around. "My gun's aimed right at her left tit."

"I'll blow your head off, you bastard," Ronan growled.

"Yep, but my finger will squeeze this trigger anyhow," Fargo said. "You shoot and I'm dead, but so's she."

"Ronan," Alicia called sharply, "put your gun down. He's not the bluffing kind."

"Smart girl," Fargo commented while he continued to hold the Colt ready to blast Alicia from the saddle. "Tell him to come around where I can see him."

"Do as he says," Alicia ordered, and he heard Ronan move through the brush and then come into sight near Alicia. Others were circling back, coming up behind Alicia, he saw.

"Everybody stays back. I've a nervous trigger finger, honey," Fargo said, and saw Alicia's beautiful face as if fashioned of ice as she peered into the bushes.

"See that they stay away, Ronan," Alicia said with authority.

Fargo waited as Ronan moved into the trees to bark orders. "Now get off the horse, Alicia," Fargo said. "We're going for a walk."

"Don't do it," Ronan called. "He could do anything."

"We're going to talk some," Fargo said.

"Don't believe him," Ronan called back.

"Shut up, Fred," Alicia said as he swung from the horse. "You're a bad judge of character." She left the horse and walked toward the brush, and Fargo rose, the Colt still aimed at her. He stepped backward, let her follow, and took the Ovaro's reins in one hand. He moved to the edge of the trees and halted, the Colt still on target.

"What made you follow?" he asked.

"We found the ark. We never found any bodies. Ronan had the men search both sides of the river, all the way down to Calkins Creek. I decided not to take any chances," Alicia said.

"Aggie and a few of the others were lucky," Fargo said. "They made it, that's all."

Alicia's slow smile held chiding contempt. "Nice try, Fargo," she said. "The goddamn sheep are with her, alive. You made that happen, somehow. She'd have gone on in her stubborn way and lost everything. But you saw to it that she didn't lose everything, damn you."

"Fishing, honey?" Fargo asked.

"I know it. If it had just been her neck saved, she'd have turned back. She'd have lost and she'd know it. But she kept on. She has the goddamn lambs. She's still going to try."

"We parted company. She's gone her way," Fargo said.

Alicia's lip curled. "Don't play me for a fool, Fargo," she snapped.

Fargo felt the tightness take hold of him. The word games were over. "Then don't be a fool," he shot back. "It'll cost you too much to keep on."

Alicia shrugged and looked coldly beautiful. "I'll find that out for myself," she said.

"You will," Fargo said, and put more certainty in the answer than he felt. He wheeled the Ovaro and sent the horse racing west in a gallop, skirted the cedars, and plunged into the woods. He stayed in the forest cover until he left the trees at least a mile on. They'd be too far back to catch him by the time Alicia returned to Ronan, but they'd try to stay on his trail and that was all he wanted for the moment. He gave them stretches of hoofprints to follow, swerved into forest and out again, leaving just enough to keep them from breaking off the pursuit. When dusk finally began to slide over the land, he reversed himself and held his path back into the trees on leaf-covered woodland ground where trailing would be a slow and painstaking task.

It was dark when he emerged back into open land

near the passage into the ravine. He'd put them off a day, but that was all he'd done, he realized. They'd go back to where he had met them and return to following the wagon tracks into the ravine. Certain and inexorable, the course of events was set. He had to find a way to change the outcome.

A lamp glowed from inside the shack as he rode into the ravine and he saw Ben and Ned step out to flank the door, rifles in their hands as they heard the hoofbeats of a horse approaching.

"Hold your fire," Fargo called, and reined to a halt to vault from the saddle. Aggie hurried from the shack, concern in her face. "Never got to look for a town," Fargo said. "But I found Alicia and all her hired guns."

Aggie's lips parted in shocking surprise. "She followed. Damn her hide, she followed," Aggie hissed.

"She's smart," Fargo said. "She won't let herself be fooled by how things look to be. Come morning, they'll find their way here. They'll come charging down the passage at us."

"It narrows. We can pick them off," Ben suggested.

"Not unless we break up their charge first, break it up so we can have time to pick them off," Fargo said.

"You've some ideas for that?" Ben queried.

"Yes. We'll put them to work at dawn. I figure it'll take them into midmorning to find us. We'll be ready and waiting as we've ever been," Fargo said. "Now get some shut-eye and be up at dawn."

The three men turned into the cabin as he unsaddled the Ovaro and took down his bedroll. Aggie came to him, walked beside him to where he set down the bedroll and started to pull off clothes. She waited till he was naked before she flung aside her things with angry motions and slid into the bedroll beside him.

"You were right again," she murmured.

"I wish I weren't," he said.

"Maybe we should pack up and run, now while it's dark," Aggie said.

"They're too near. They'd see our tracks, come morning, and catch us someplace maybe impossible to defend," Fargo said. "This is it, Aggie—win, lose, or draw."

She pressed herself tight against him. "Hold me, Skye, just hold me," she murmured, and he wrapped his arms around her small form until she fell asleep. He turned on his side, and she didn't wake from her still and silent hiding place.

He slept with her, plans forming in his mind. They were simple enough and he could only hope they worked. When dawn touched the sky with pink fingers, he woke, shook Aggie awake, and pulled on clothes at once. By the time Aggie finished dressing he had his lariat in hand and saw Ben emerge from the cabin. Zeke and Ned followed a few moments later and Fargo held the lariat up in one hand. "Get all the heavy clothesline we have," he said.

"There's some extra lariat in the wagon toolbox," Ben said, and hurried to fetch the rope.

Fargo motioned to him to follow when he started back with the extra rope and led the way to the mouth of the narrowed section of the passage. He tied the end of two lengths of rope to the base of two thin alders and stretched it across the ground of the passageway to two more trees on the other side. He let the rope lay limp on the ground and saw Ben nod in understanding.

"Trip ropes," Ben said. "They won't be expecting that."

"I'm counting on that. You three stay hidden on that side. Aggie will stay here with me," Fargo said, and turned to Aggie beside him. "You'll take one rope and I'll take the other. When I give the signal you pull yours taut and wrap it around the tree next to you. I'll be doing the same with mine."

"Got it." She nodded.

Fargo squinted up at the passage between the rocks. "They'll be charging in to catch us before we've a chance to run. The first horses will hit the ropes and go down and those behind will fall over them. More than half ought to pile up and go down before the others can rein up. You start shooting as soon as the first ones hit the ground. We'll have Ronan and his men down and in a cross fire."

"It'll work," Aggie said. "It's got to work."

"Now fetch your rifles and come back here and wait," Fargo said as he straightened up and strode back to the Ovaro beside the house. He took the big Sharps, saw Aggie lift a heavy Spencer from the supply box beneath the wagon. Zeke, Ben, and Ned came from the shack with their guns and followed Fargo back to the waiting place at the foot of the passage.

Fargo pulled Aggie behind a low rock with him, set his rifle on the ground, and wrapped the end of the rope around his hand. Aggie followed his example and he peered across the passage. Ben, Zeke, and Ned had hunkered down well out of sight, he saw with satisfaction.

"How long before they get here?" Aggie whispered.

Fargo glanced up at the sky, which had begun to spread the flush of the morning sun. "Soon enough," he murmured. "Soon enough." He leaned back, relaxed, and kept the end of the rope in his hand. Aggie rested her head against his shoulder as the morning grew full and warm. He glanced down at her and saw her quiet calmness belied by the tense set of her jaw and the tiny lines that pulled at her mouth.

He glimpsed the sun moving high into the sky, and he had just shifted position when he heard the hoofbeats. Aggie shot a quick glance at him, her eyes wide, and he listened to the hoofbeats come to a halt at the top of the passage. They could see the shack and the other two structures from there and they could perhaps hear the lambs bleating for food. The sound would surely send them into action, proof that they had found their quarry.

Fargo counted off seconds and suddenly the stillness exploded with the thunder of galloping hooves. He shifted position to where he could see from between two rocks. The thunder of hooves grew louder and the first row of riders came into sight, Ronan in the lead. They were going full out, four in the first row, at least five more close on their heels.

"Ready," he whispered to Aggie, and she nodded. He closed his hand around the rope that stretched unseen on the ground, waited another fifteen seconds, his eye on the horses' legs. "Now," he rasped out, his voice a coarse whisper as he yanked his rope and the line came taut some seven or eight inches above the ground.

He glimpsed Aggie's rope stretch tight a foot away from his, but he rushed to wrap the end of the lariat around the tree. He took a half-dozen turns with it and saw Aggie frantically doing the same with hers. Shouts filled the air and he saw the ropes quiver violently as the horses slammed into them. He scooped the Sharps into his hands, poked it through a crevice between two rocks, and looked at the pileup of falling horses and men directly in front of him. The first volley of shots exploded from across the passage and he saw two men fall as they tried to regain their feet. He picked out a figure trying to avoid being struck by a horse falling just behind him. He fired and the man stumbled forward and lay still.

Shouts, curses, the snorted sounds of horses rearing, falling, and regaining their feet became a wild obbligato to the drumbeat of rifle fire, and Fargo sighted on two figures trying to scramble up the passageway, fired, and both men fell as one. The gunhands who had managed to rein up had turned their horses in the narrow passages amid colliding rumps and shouted oaths and were fleeing, he saw, as the rifle fire from the other side finished another two figures scrambling for safety. As some of the riderless horses ran up the narrow passage, others streaked into the ravine in aimless confusion, and suddenly the narrow mouth of the passage was a silent place.

Fargo rose, stepped from behind the rocks, and felt Aggie at his heels. He counted the still forms that littered the ground as he stepped among them. "Ten," he grunted as Ben and the others came out. "That leaves eleven more, counting Alicia. We cut them down by about half."

"Will they attack again?" Aggie asked.

"Not right away. They've been hurt bad," Fargo said as he surveyed the bodies again. Ronan was not among them, he noted. The man had managed to escape, though he was leading the charge.

"Christ, we have to bury this whole lot?" Ned asked.

"We'll put them in the wagon and take them off someplace, come dark," Fargo said. "Unless Alicia sends someone for them."

"Not likely," Aggie put in. "They're nothing to her, disposable objects."

"Then we'll take care of it tonight. We'll post sentry duty from tonight on. We'll take shifts, but I want someone right here at the foot of the passage at all times," Fargo said. "Now let's get back to our own chores." He led the way back to the houses, and Ned and Ben rode off to the far side of the ravine and began the slow business of cutting down trees for new roof and wall planking. Ned carried the chalk line, Fargo noted, and he concentrated his own efforts on sawing the existing roof timbers where they'd broken into clean, straight ends so they could be joined to the new ones with stout pegs.

It was always backbreaking work building a shelter, and by night Ben and Ned returned with only a few lengths of hewn and squared-off timber. But it was a beginning, and there might have been a celebration if everyone had not been so tired.

Fargo divided sentry duty into three-hour shifts so everyone could get some sleep. He took the first shift himself. Ned spelled him when it was over, and he had Ben go with him in the wagon to carry the slain gunhands to the far end of the ravine. They dug a wide and shallow grave and put the bodies in it, covered it with logs and loose stone and the earth they'd shoveled out. Aggie had insisted on taking sentry along with everyone else and she was on duty when he returned with Ben. He took his bedroll off to the side, undressed, and slept almost at once. He woke only when Aggie came, crawled in beside him, and slept wrapped tightly around him.

When morning came, Fargo rode out into the passage, climbed up between the rocks, and surveyed the plateau. Only the herds of wild horses met his gaze, again stretching far across the flat, grassy land, occasionally exploding into bursts of galloping energy that took them in and out between the rock formations. He rode down the passage with a frown creased across his brow, and settled the debate within himself by the time he reached the shack and the others had just finished coffee. "We'll take three-hour shifts again through the day but with a variation. Sentry duty will be at the top of the passage by day. You see them heading this way, you sound the alarm. That'll give us all a chance to get in position in the rocks before they come down."

"I'll start," Aggie said. "Ben and Ned need the daylight to chop and hew. I can cook and clean by night if I have to."

Fargo nodded agreement, assigned the other shifts, and watched Aggie ride up the narrow passage with the big Spencer in one hand. The day went quickly and quietly and he shot two more rabbits for the dinner pot. Ben had them skinned and cleaned and ready for Aggie's hand before dusk set in.

"Maybe she's finally given up," Aggie said over supper. Fargo shot her a skeptical glance and she shrugged. "I guess not," she muttered. "That's not Alicia."

"It's not you, either," he commented, and drew a quick glare. But when he put his bedroll out later on, she was there. As the night grew long, he woke to the sweet touch of her lips moving up and down his body. She made love to him with a new urgency that took him by surprise, discovery replaced by devouring need, and the moon was high when her last scream of pleasure curled upward and she fell exhausted beside him.

Morning came and he rose, washed, and dressed as she took her time waking. He had the first day shift and he rode the pinto to the top of the passage. The herds were moving acros the plateau with the new day and he watched two magnificent stallions lead a harem of mares and fillies in a run across the far end of the plain. As his gaze slowly scanned the land, it came to a sudden halt on the lone rider that slowly moved toward him, full black hair glistening, long breasts swaying as she rode.

Alicia made her way across and halted in front of him, her black-brown eyes searching his face. "Came to talk," she said.

"I'm here," he grunted.

She drew a deep sigh and her breasts pushed hard against the white shirt. She seemed resigned. "You were right," she said. "It's costing too much to keep on." He felt his thick brows lift in surprise.

"You giving up?" He frowned.

"Yes," Alicia said. "I still don't think she'll make it through the winter. You can't do anything clever to keep the blizzards away."

"No, I can't," he said.

"Besides, I'm not going back empty-handed," Alicia said. "She can keep her damn lambs. I've found something much better." Fargo frowned and she turned

149

in the saddle and gestured to the wild herds across the plateau. "I've enough men left to round a fair-size herd up and drive them back with us," Alicia said.

"That'll be damn hard to do," Fargo said.

"We can do it. We'll use a rope corral and be careful. With this stock as breeding foundation I'll make a damn fortune," Alicia said. "We'll start with a lot more than we can handle and expect to lose half along the way. But we'll hang on to the others."

"You've some other reason for telling me all this," Fargo said.

"Yes. I don't want you picking off my boys if they're chasing down a horse too near your passage into the ravine," she said.

"You calling a truce?" Fargo asked.

"Guess that's as good a name as any. We're going to be corralling horses, that's all. The rest is over. No more shooting," Alicia said. "Aggie can play with her lambs. I'll take care of my horses."

"Fair enough," Fargo agreed.

She turned, paused, and looked back. "My offer to you is still good, Fargo," she said.

"I'll remember that," he told her, and watched her ride away before he returned to the others. He told them what Alicia had said and Aggie breathed a deep sigh.

"I won," she said. "I won."

"So far," Ben said. "Let's wait till spring to celebrate."

"What are you thinking now?" Aggie asked Fargo as she read the furrow on his brow.

"Seems like a sudden attack of common sense for Alicia," he commented.

"She's seen greener grass, the mustangs. That's Alicia," Aggie said.

Fargo shrugged and set aside the tiny questions that stirred inside him. He helped Ben bring newly cut timber close to the house and kept himself busy until night fell.

With Aggie beside him he slept the night away and the next morning he rode to the top of the passage and gazed across the plateau. Alicia, Ronan, and the rest of her men were busy rounding up wild horses. They had set up a rope corral with stakes pushed into the ground and he saw a dozen mustangs already inside its confines. The lower end of the corral ended not more than a few dozen yards from the top of the passage, he noted. One man tended to the rope entrance, and when another three or four horses were driven in, he'd close the rope door. Fargo watched the horses wheel and mill inside the rope corral. Horses being herd animals, it was their nature to band together in the face of the new and the unknown. The ropes were both, and unless they were frightened, they'd stay inside the confines of the rope.

He watched a spell longer and finally returned to the ravine below. He paid another visit just before the day closed and saw two men were riding in slow circles around the perimeter of the makeshift corral while the others bedded down in the distance. When he returned to the shack, Aggie and the others waited eagerly.

"They're rounding up a big herd," Fargo said. "We'll still post sentries for the night."

"No need," Aggie said. "I know Alicia. Once she's given up, she's through."

"Three-hour shifts," Fargo said. "Same rotation."

Aggie made a face at him but went out to get a jacket as the night wind grew chilly. He took the first shift and she was asleep in the bedroll when he returned. She rolled against him the moment he slid in beside her and clung to him the rest of the night.

When morning came, he rode up to the plateau and watched as the roundup continued. He saw Ronan work a young blaze-faced filly into the rope corral, and the man shot a brooding glance at him. Fargo returned to the work waiting below and kept wondering why the uneasiness continued to stab at him. They were plainly rounding up the wild stock, all their efforts channeled into the task. Even Alicia had helped as he watched. Maybe he was a pessimist, he frowned as he carried a long piece of cut and hewn timber to the house. But he rode up again in the late afternoon and left Ben and Ned measuring beam lengths to replace the broken corner of the roof and Zeke helping Aggie feed the lambs.

He reached the top of the passage and stared at the horses that had been herded into the top corral. At least fifty, he guessed, perhaps seventy-five. Too many to drive back, far too many, he frowned. They'd be lucky to have fifteen or twenty left. They were all plainly amateurs at driving horses, he decided, and his gaze spotted Alicia, Ronan, and the rest of his men at the far end of their makeshift corral. The rope entranceway had been tied loosely closed against one of the thin posts in the ground, but the herd instinctively stayed away from the ropes. They stayed together in a long line inside the rope corral and he saw at least two stallions among the mustangs they'd gathered.

There was another hour of daylight left and he was about to turn back down the passage when he saw Ronan bring his horse out alongside the rope line. The other man followed to form a line along the back of the horses inside. He felt the frown on his brow turn into a whispered curse as Ronan drew his gun, fired three times in the air, and the others began to set off a hail of shots behind the horses. At one, the wild horses began to surge forward. They were into a gallop in split seconds, and Fargo saw Ronan and his men race alongside the herd, firing into the air. He felt the curse well up inside him, fight its way to his throat, and spew into the air. "Goddamn her. Goddamn her lying bitchy hide," Fargo roared. They were stampeding the horses, driving them into the passage. He held frozen for a moment as he watched the thundering mass of flying hooves come at him, nearly a hundred panic-filled, raging, wild horses, bent only on charging forward, trampling everything in their path. The rope corral flew aside as though it didn't exist, and Fargo wheeled the Ovaro in a tight circle and raced down the passage into the ravine.

"Run," he yelled as he galloped toward the houses. "Get your horses. Run."

Aggie stared at him, frozen to the spot, and Zeke and Ned headed for the wagon.

"Stampede," Fargo screamed, not that there was any need to, for the first of the wild horses had already burst through the passage, the others at their heels. He saw Ronan's men spread out on both sides, firing, keeping the stampeding horses together in a straight line. He saw Ben running for the gelding, but Aggie seemed transfixed, her eyes staring in horror at the onrushing stampede of horseflesh. Fargo reached her, leaned over, and tried to get an arm around her waist. "Here, dammit. Run," he yelled, but she pulled away from him.

"The lambs," she said. "I've got to save the lambs."

"No, there's no time," he yelled, but she was already running toward the small, open-ended barn. He flicked a glance up at the stampeding horses and saw their wild eyes and flying manes only a few yards away. He spurred the Ovaro forward, leaned down, and caught hold of Aggie as she was about to run into where the lambs were loose on the barn floor.

"No," she screamed as he lifted her, swung her up and across the saddle facedown. "I can save them," she cried out, and tried to turn, scratch at him, and slide from the Ovaro. He slammed her down again, brought his hand around, and slapped her hard across the face. She cried out and began to sob as he wheeled the Ovaro, looked over his shoulder, and saw at least fifteen charging, mindless, enraged, and panic-filled horses only a dozen feet away. They were already trampling the storage shed into the ground and he decided they were too close to outrace. He veered to the right, raced beside the main house, and turned right again as he drew his Colt. Ronan rode alongside the stampeding mustangs, firing to keep them in line. Fargo aimed quickly, pulled the trigger on the Colt, and Ronan seemed to buck in the saddle without his horse bucking. He rose up, twisted, and spurted a stream of red from just under his neck. Fargo saw him fall in a twisting motion as he raced the Ovaro past him.

He bent low in the saddle, leaned across Aggie's back, and raced the Ovaro for the side of the ravine. He didn't have to look back. The sound of planking being smashed in and crushed all but filled the air. It almost drowned out the mercifully quick, high-pitched bleats of the lambs as they were trampled into the ground. When he reached the side of the ravine, he raced the Ovaro into the buckeyes, reined up sharply, and slid to the ground. Aggie slid down, half-collapsed, and he heard the racking sobs that shook her small form. He drew the rifle from its saddle case and went down on one knee at the edge of the trees. He gazed across at the still-stampeding herd which now began to stretch out as Alicia's men stopped firing. He saw the wagon on its side, much of it smashed into the ground. The storage shed had only one wall left attached to the shack and the shack itself leaned as if blown by a terrible wind.

Fargo glimpsed Alicia, her horse halted beside Ronan's body, two more riders with her. Four others started toward him, riding hard for the side of the ravine. Aggie's racking sobs continued behind him as he raised the rifle, waited, let the men come in closer. He took out the first two instantly, missed the third one as the man dived from the horse. The fourth one made the error of turning to flee. He never got the horse completely turned as Fargo's shot blew the back of his head in two. Fargo saw the last one on the ground roll, come up with his gun in hand and fire wildly into the trees. Fargo ducked his head as bullets spattered the buckeye and smashed into the low branches. He drew careful aim as the man disdained trying to reload and drew another pistol from his belt. Fargo's shot slammed into the man where the pistol had been, and he saw the attacker double-over, clutch both hands to his waist, and topple forward onto the ground. He groaned in pain, tried to rise, fell forward again, and lay still.

Fargo's eyes went to Alicia. She was out of range of even the big Sharps, and he cursed softly. She'd never given up. She'd conned him into believing her, had gone through all the motions. "Goddamn lying little bitch," he muttered.

Aggie's sobs still drifted to him and he swore again. She'd been stubbornly wrong for most of it, but the final right was hers and he remembered what she'd said when they first met. He'd asked if she really thought Alicia would try to kill her own sister, and Aggie had answered yes without hesitation.

He rose to his feet and watched as Alicia turned her horse and started for the passageway. He saw only two men go with her and then he spotted the forms trampled on the ground a half-dozen yards away: three of her hired hands who had miscalculated or hadn't been quick enough when the stampede swerved. His eyes returned to Alicia and he swore silently. She had reached the mouth of the passageway when the two shots rang out and Fargo's eyes widened as he saw the two men go down as one. Alicia flattened herself low on her mount and charged up the passage and out of sight, and Fargo, frowning, saw Ben emerge from behind the rocks, the rifle in his hand.

Fargo turned and strode back to Aggie. The racking sobs had finally stopped, but her eyes were saucers of pain as she looked up at him. He pulled her to her feet and she swallowed and wiped a hand across her face. "You couldn't have saved them," he said, reading the hurt and accusation in her eyes. "You'd be back there trampled into the ground with them."

She stared back, closed her eyes, and her face fell into his chest. She walked from the trees with both arms wrapped around his waist, clinging to him as though she would fall at any moment. The Ovaro followed and Fargo saw Ben come down from the passage and halt beside the crushed and splintered wagon. He started at the two bodies inside it for a long moment and finally turned away. "They shouldn't have gone to the wagon. They just shouldn't have," Ben said. "But then what do river men know about a stampede?"

"Glad you made it through, Ben," Fargo said.

"Ned and Zeke weren't paying any mind to me," Ben said. "I got two of the ones who ended up crushed on the ground, and raced back to the rocks by the passage. I was waiting there when she came by with the last two." He looked at Aggie and put one hand on the close-cropped hair. "It's done. You tried, Aggie. You can't do more than try," he said gently.

"I tried and she won," Aggie said bitterly. "She won."

Fargo put one hand under her chin and lifted her face to his. "It happens, Aggie," he said. "The good guys don't always win."

She took in his words and turned her face away after a long moment. Fargo saw small clusters of the mustangs move out of the ravine and up the passage. "Get the gelding, Ben," he said. "Let's get out of here. There's nothing left we can do and no reason to stay around."

The older man nodded and walked back to where he'd left the horse hidden at the bottom of the passage. Fargo half-lifted Aggie onto the Ovaro and swung on behind her. Dusk was settling over the land when he reached the plateau above, and the night came soon after. More as matter of habit than anything else, he noted the lone prints of Alicia's horse as she headed south.

Aggie rode in silence, and when dark fell and he found a spot to camp, she remained silent. They ate cold beef jerky with no pleasure in it, and when he lay down, Aggie lay beside him, not touching him. She stayed wrapped in silence and he let her sleep with her own pain and her own thoughts. It'd take time for her, he realized. Her stubbornness wouldn't accept defeat easily. He closed his eyes and slept, an inner tiredness adding itself to the outer one.

It was morning when he woke, the sun bright, and he glanced at Aggie and felt the oath leap from his lips. She wasn't there and he bounced to his feet, his eyes seeking the gelding, and found the horse was gone too. Ben sat up, fought sleep out of his face. "Goddamn her, she's gone," Fargo bit out.

"Gone where?" Ben asked.

"Where do you think? After Alicia," Fargo roared as he vaulted onto the Ovaro. "Start walking. You'll catch up to us in time," he tossed at Ben as he sent the pinto off in a gallop.

The gelding's prints were fresh, following on the heels of Alicia's horse, and Fargo swore again as he rode. She'd probably left before dawn, moved carefully until the first light let her pick up the prints. But she hadn't that much of a head start and he thanked the Lord for small favors.

The trail turned and he spotted a grove of alder at the far end of the plateau. The prints led directly into the trees and Fargo slowed the Ovaro, leapt to the ground, and raced to one side in his long, crouching lope. He plunged silently into the trees and came up around the back, guessed at the spot where the prints had gone into the trees. He moved quickly on cat's feet, staying on the balls of his feet as he crept forward. He heard the voices, cut to the right, and saw Aggie first, standing almost directly in front of him. He saw Alicia as he pushed aside a low-hanging branch.

The two young women faced each other and he saw Aggie held a Smith & Wesson Model One in her hand. Alicia held a long-barreled single-action Colt Navy model pistol in her hand, her shirt unbuttoned and hanging out and her hair disheveled. Somehow, she still managed to look coldly beautiful.

"You don't deserve to live, Alicia," he heard Aggie say.

"You shoot, I'll shoot," Alicia said. "You're being stubborn and stupid again, as usual."

"Maybe it's worth it, this time," Aggie said.

Fargo edged another step closer and drew his own Colt.

"You lost. This won't make you win," Alicia said.

"No, it won't," Aggie agreed, and a sadness touched her voice. "But you won't win either, and I'll feel better for that. So will Pa."

"Stupid, you're stupid," Alicia bit out. "You never could win. You never knew how to win, and this isn't winning now. You're just too stupid to know it, sister dear."

Fargo grimaced. It was all personal now, Alicia drawing on her icy ruthlessness and Aggie working out of the bitterness and her sense of injustice. They were too close to each other to miss if they fired, and the first shot would trigger the second. Aggie's life hung on a very slender thread of her own making. She hadn't reasoned, hadn't thought it out. Or maybe she had, Fargo pondered. Pain and hurt brought her here, the past and the present.

Fargo's finger lay against the trigger of the Colt. If he had to shoot one of them, it'd be Alicia. She had tried to kill him, Aggie, and everyone else in her way. But if he fired, the shot would make them both pull their triggers and it would all end in tragedy.

He needed a distraction, something to break Aggie's

concentration and do the same for Alicia, something to make them turn away from their confrontation with death. He needed it damn quickly, he knew. He moved, circled silently, and came up behind Alicia. He stayed low in the brush till he was directly behind her, and when he stood up, he saw Aggie's eyes widen in surprise as she spied him.

Alicia saw her eyes grow wide too, and she whirled instantly, her gun ready to fire, and Fargo let the Colt explode in a single shot. Alicia's gun flew from her hand and she gasped in pain. But the moment had been broken, the spell snapped, and Aggie's finger hadn't tightened on the trigger.

"Goddamn you," Alicia screamed, and flew at him.

He ducked, seized her by the arm, twisted, and sent her flying into a tree. She slammed into the hard bark and slid to the ground in a daze. It'd take her a spell to recover, he knew, and he walked to where Aggie still held the gun in her hand.

He reached out and she let him take the gun. "Let's go," he said, and she turned with him with quiet obedience that was not really obedience, he knew, but the result of the emotional fatigue.

"You should've let me," Aggie muttered.

"You couldn't live with having killed your sister," he said. "She could, but not you."

"I wasn't planning on living with it," Aggie said.

"Dumb," he bit out. "I've better plans for you."

He took the gelding by the reins and led the horse out of the trees and climbed onto the pinto with Aggie.

"The good guys don't always win," she murmured with bitterness.

"That's right," he said. "But they can live to go on, maybe win next time around."

He saw the hope spring into her eyes. "Yes, maybe next time around," she said. "Will you be there?"

"Not likely," he said. "But I plan to stay awhile now."

"I'll settle for that," Aggie said, and her lips came up to his. They stayed, sweet wanting, as he rode on.

LOOKING FORWARD!

The following is the opening
section from the next novel in the exciting
Trailsman series from Signet:

THE TRAILSMAN #66
TREACHERY PASS

*Idaho Territory. Late autumn, 1861,
winter already whispering along the
Oregon Trail—that rutted, bloodstained
wilderness route that killed or cured . . .*

The two puffs of smoke had quickly turned to pale-blue rings, slowly blowing through the mud-chinked windows in the rear wall of the long room. The shrieks and bellows of half-drunken song, the wailing of fiddles, and the pounding of dancing feet had suddenly stopped. The participants could only stand and gape, amazed at the two fast shots that had so suddenly and unexpectedly turned the gaiety into silence.

However, Fat Dan's Grand Slam Casino was used to such upsets. A large, square building of mud, log, and stone, it perched on the south bank of the Snake River with the dozen or so other structures comprising Glenns Ferry. The settlement was well-located to serve as a trading post and a natural stop along the Oregon Trail, which forded the Snake here to continue northwestward. Fat Dan's was among the first, begun in the '40s as an honest tavern, changing owners and names, but growing steadily on into those hectic '50s, its notoriety growing with it, until it had become one of the most dangerous dives on the far frontier. But despite all it had seen, this latest shooting had been swift enough to make men's hair stand on end.

Across the table in the left-rear corner, a burly gambler lay sprawled forward, his whiskery face resting in a large pile of gold coins and poker chips. Five rumpled cards were tightly gripped in his left hand, the right hand still a balled fist around the cow-horned butt of a double-barreled German pistol.

Against the wall stood the dead gambler's opponent, smoking Cole revolver in hand, calmly viewing the situation. "Counting the joker, a man might have five, but hell if there's a poker deck that packs six aces." His tone lifted only slightly as he glanced toward the long, hewn-log bar. "Houseman, cash me in. One thousand four hundred dollars, in gold. I'm not fond of picture money."

There was no answer for at least ten seconds. Fat Dan's manager and cashier stood by the bar as if transfixed, a slight, thin gray-bearded man who knew he was damned if he did and damned if he didn't. Death rarely struck just one blow in the Grand Slam Casino. Gazing at the balcony above the bar, he called with relief, "Well, Mr. Tobin?"

Men from the Missouri to the mouth of the Columbia River had heard of Fat Dan Tobin. Fortyish, he was big of bone and flesh like his name, his jowled face sporting a mustache and goatee of the same graying brown as his greasily plastered hair. On his way downstairs when the gunplay erupted, he'd thrust a pudgy hand inside his broadcloth suit coat as if to draw a shoulder-holstered hideout pistol. Removing his hand, he gave the manager a nod and finished his ponderous descent.

The dead gambler was almost as well-known. Many men had tangled with Slick Dudley, who was sharp and shrewd when it came to cards, dice, or wheel, and rumor was that in the two years he'd run Fat Dan's games, Dudley had killed at least a dozen fools who'd bucked his play.

It was impossible that such an operator should die so quickly at the hands of this stranger. He was black-haired and bearded, his chiseled features darkened by wind and sun, his eyes a cold lake-blue that even in this moment of deadly confrontation held an intent reticence, suggesting that he preferred to stand apart. As it was, he stood tall in workaday garb and a buck-skin jacket, lean and hard, latent power evident in the relaxed slope of his shoulders. He looked what he was: a rough-hewn, durable, self-sufficient frontiers-man—not a backwoods yokel, but not a professional cardsharp or gunslinger either.

Fat Dan Tobin seemed to be taking the stranger's measure, one hand on the staircase post, the other tugging his goatee. Then, after a quick scan around, he spoke in a lazy drawl, devoid of any excitement. "You're wantin' a lot of money, pal. What seemed to be the hassle between you'n Slick Dudley?"

"Too many aces." The stranger's lips twitched as if about to smile. "I caught him three times in a row. He has cards up either sleeve, and I don't know how many you'll find inside his hat. You can shake him down in your leisure. I've said I'm cashing in."

"And yuh called 'im," Tobin replied, ignoring the last remark, "or did yuh just shoot 'im under the table without callin'?"

"I called him. He saw he was trapped and went for his pistol."

"I still say one thousand and four hundred is a lot of money."

"The chips on the table will bear me out." A low hardening was creeping into the stranger's tone. "The deck, the cards in his hand, in his sleeves, and in his hat will prove the rest of it. When you check our hands you'll find that I held a pair of aces and three queens. Slick still holds the king of spades—and four aces."

"Plum interestin', if true." Tobin licked his lips, and again there was silence, faintly broken here and there by the scrape of a boot as the crowd kept easing back to make room. Many of the women who had been dancing or cadging drinks at the bar had already turned and noiselessly scooted away to safer spots. They knew, as did the men, that gunfire would come again, fast and furious, if Fat Dan gave the signal.

One curvaceous wench, though, abruptly deserted her grizzled customer and hurried toward the stairs, her face pale beneath her makeup. She rushed up to Tobin, throwing herself between him and the stranger as she leaned forward, her words intended for a whisper, but they came out as a sharp hiss that carried around the room. "Go easy, honey! Yakima Flynn just told me that man is—"

"Shuddup, Velvet," Tobin growled, shoving her aside and addressing the stranger with a mocking sneer. "Pal, if you'd let Slick Dudley live, we might've settled this thing with no loss o' time. But, hell, I ain't about to pay out my good money just 'cause some hotshot kills a gambler at one o' my tables, then rises to make his demand."

As Tobin spoke, the stranger pivoted and triggered his revolver. Another pistol blazed fire across the room, the twin reports drowning out a howl of pain as the casino bouncer reeled against the bar, pawing at his bloodied hand. The long-barreled Adams .44 he'd stealthily drawn clattered to the floor from nerveless fingers, the web of his thumb and much of his palm skewered by lead.

"You're handy, m' friend," Tobin said thickly, then scowled at the woman he'd called Velvet. "Okay, who is he?"

"Skye Fargo."

"Fargo." Tobin regarded the man, tugging his goatee again. "I heard tell o' you. Scout an' pilot for a bunch o' the wagon trains that rolled the trail, weren't you? Raised hell with the Injuns and hard cases around Fort Hall."

"I was there." Fargo's tone was hardening. "Now I'm here, and I'm waiting for my money."

"Wal, 'course, if yuh'd made yourself known, sir, no sech misunderstandin' would've ever happened. Not in any place o' mine." Tobin strode to the poker table, making a good show of it, knowing all eyes were on him. With one swift kick he sent the chair flying from under the dead gambler. Slick Dudley's body pitched backward in a loose flop that sprawled itself flat on the floor, arms thrown out, a flutter of cards flying from the sleeves. He stepped astride, the corpse and picked up the fine beaver hat, dug a big fist into it, and swore.

"Hell!" he roared, spilling card after card from inside the hat and tossing it down. "The damn topper's got a double linin' and was stuffed full. Cash Mist' Fargo in, Proust, and have the boys boothill bury this cheatin' carcass. I run an honest house!" As the manager came hustling, Tobin glared at the crowd as if seeking at least a flicker of confirmation from somebody. "Honest Daniel! That's what they used to call me in Kansas. Belly to the bar, folks, the house is buyin' a round. I'll show yuh how big a sport Honest Dan Tobin can be." With that, he stomped back upstairs to his balcony office.

Fargo was relieved, doubting he could have shot his way clear. He wasn't surprised, though, figuring Tobin's agreeable mood had nothing to do with being honest or a sport, but with getting even and back in control. Might made right on this wild frontier, and a crafty owner of a dive like Fat Dan's would try to gain a hold over anyone strong and skilled. Tobin had simply made a calculated move to whip Fargo into his hands, aware—as Fargo was aware—that a man who would take money, even with the excuse of having won it gambling, was frequently a man who could be handled, shaped, and forced to fight as he was told.

Nor was Fargo surprised to see Velvet start to sidle across the room. The manager, Proust, was piling gold coins on the next table, interested solely in exact counting. But money and power often held a strange fascination for those who plied avaricious trades, and true to type, Velvet was gazing avidly at the stacks as she eased closer, her hand sliding back and forth over her hip.

He kept an eye on her advance while helping Proust sack the money in a canvas string bag, until a man approached and doffed his hat. "M'name's Wyndam, Otis Wyndam. I'm with the wagon train that pulled in this evening. May I set?"

Fargo shrugged and Wyndam settled in a nearby chair, a solid, stout chap of mid-thirties, with one of those homely, frank faces people instinctively trust. He had thinning hair neatly combed, a persuasively earnest voice, and wore plain denims and a butternut shirt; in fact, the loudest thing about him was his hat: a flat sombrero with a braided rattlesnake band, four silver tinsel stars on the crown and four on the underside of the brim. He promptly began a conversation, to which Fargo at first paid only peripheral attention.

"Did I o'erhear correctly, Mr. Fargo, that you're a scout? Yes? And that you've trekked the trail?"

"A time or two, yes."

"Beyond it, far as the Willamette Valley?"

"South of Portland?" Fargo nodded. "Rich farmland."

"The finest. Sixty- or one-hundred-sixty-acre tracts, that's my offer to every pilgrim willing to follow me to Oregon City. Virgin soil, deep and fertile, right on the river for transportation, the perfect place to settle new homes. Uh-huh, and the niggardly sum of a dollar an acre is all I'm asking."

"All paid in advance, too, I reckon."

"Ah, well, in this case seeing is believing."

Wyndam choked, Velvet having suddenly intervened with an undulating thrust of her pelvis. Fargo grinned. In her early twenties, he judged, she was in precious little else. Her red spangled dance-hall costume fit like an hourglass corset. She had doe eyes that said she had never loved anyone passionately in her life, and a bee-stung mouth that made liars out of them, especially when she cozied up and planted a kiss on Fargo.

Velvet flashed a saucy look at the openmouthed spectators. "The custom here's for a man to give the girl who kisses him a present, isn't it?" Returning to Fargo she said, "I'm ready to claim mine, please."

Without a word Fargo pulled Velvet tightly against him and pressed his lips to hers, warmly, lingeringly.

When he released her, she wobbled back a pace and clapped a hand over her breasts, partly because she was gasping for breath and partly because Fargo had discreetly dropped four gold coins down her cleavage during their embrace. A chorus of hoots and guffaws erupted. An embarrassed flush brightening her rouged cheeks, Velvet burrowed through the hurrahing crowd to make a quick getaway out a side door.

Chuckling, Fargo wedged the cash bag behind his belt and was tucking in his shirt when he saw Wyndam glance obliquely at the front entrance. Following, he glimpsed a large, rawboned man in a long frock coat and black slouch hat of the sort worn by parsons. Shocks of white hair showed under the brim, and a wide mattress of beard spread down his brawny bosom, almost bristling as he glowered with righteous condemnation.

When Wyndam faced Fargo again, he realized Skye had caught his glance and laughed softly, waving his hand. "That's Brigham Blutcher, a member of our train. He doesn't approve of this, or of you." Wyndam paused, thoughtfully studying Fargo. "You're a fiddle-foot rogue, but there's more to you than that. I don't miss on many folks. It's my guess that once you agree to a job, you'd stick through to finish it, come Satan or high water. Am I right?"

"If I can. If the job's as agreed." A faint suspiciousness edged his voice. "You aren't hinting your train needs to hire a pilot, are you?"

"Nope." I can guide okay, and our second section is bossed by an ex-teamster who knows the ropes and follows m' lead well. Tremayne's his name. Give him a howdy for me, will you, if you're here when he pulls in next week."

Fargo scowled. "No train has sections strung a week apart."

"It kinda developed. More folks joined than I bargained for, almost forty wagons. Enough to form two sections, luckily, 'cause feuding grew hot 'tween those not ready to leave and thems unwilling to wait. Leaders we got plenty of," Wyndam added, a harried sigh. "I thought p'raps we might take you on as a wing scout."

"Forget it. If you're smart, forget going at all. You're too late, the season's gone, and signs point to an early, stormy winter. Don't bet your lives on reaching Oregon City before heavy snows block the Blue Mountains or ice blizzards trap you along the Columbia Gorge."

"We don't intend to. I've got copies of maps Gen'ral Stevens drew when he explored overland to the Pacific Northwest. Detouring on his route will bypass the Gorge and Deadman's Pass, and cut a hundred miles or more off the regular trail—"

Fargo tensed, mouth clamped, eyes narrowing speculatively.

"—Still, time is pressing. But so are we, and barring any major delay, I expect we'll succeed." Wyndam finished confidently, then waved the thought away as if it was unimportant. "But this isn't what I wanted to talk to you about. We've had some trouble and we'll have some more. I need a man who can handle vermin the way you just did. It's worth high dollar to me."

Fargo shook his head. "I'm pulling out in the morning."

"Westbound?"

"Wyoming, the Teton Basin." Fargo turned to go with a parting nod. "I hope your train, both halves, makes it across."

Talk had premanently resumed in the casino, but it died again as Fargo pushed through the crowd toward the big front door. There on the threshhold loomed Brigham Blutcher, who straightened and sniffed audibly.

"I seen you. Boozin', gamblin', lechin', spillin' blood!

I seen your bloody hands," Blutcher accused dourly. "Beware! The wages of sin is death."

Fargo smiled. "Sure. But you saw me all wrong. I was just helping a certain tinhorn collect what he'd earned."

Outside, the night was cloudy dark, the only illumination coming from lamplit windows. Fargo headed warily along the street toward the local rooming house, pausing in a black-shrouded alleyway to reload and scan ahead for ambushes. Most likely Fat Dan Tobin had a fast recovery scheme cooked up, and a tavern full of hard-ass jiggers also knew what and how he'd won. Instead of reholstering his revolver, Fargo stuck it in his belt to one side of his money bag, butt forward in a loose, left-handed cross-draw position.

Moving on, he passed a few men, none of them close by and none appearing to be taking any special interest in him. He paused again when he reached the lane that led to the rooming house. Hearing nothing, seeing nothing in the gloom, Fargo began down the fetid, narrow alley with utmost caution. It was flanked by hovels and shacks that were mostly dark and silent, although an occasional glimmering window and muffled hum of voices denoted occupancy. Plenty of nooks and doorways and spaces between the shanties provided a killer a place to hide in wait.

He caught no sound, no flicker of motion. Yet danger was here, deadly, silkily whispered danger. The premonition was strong—and proved to be right.

Fargo was halfway down the lane when a shadowy figure leapt out of an alcove doorway ten yards ahead, aiming a sawed-off rifle and snarling loudly, "Fork it over, asshole, or I'll blow you to smithereens!"

As he halted, Fargo swiftly analyzed his chances and decided they were lousy. He grimaced, and it was then he heard a quick, light step behind him. Whirling, he glimpsed another man looming over him from out a concealed side doorway, his arm raised, gripping a butcher knife. That slashed his odds from lousy to zero, which meant Fargo had nothing to lose.

With a sharp twisting of his body to the left, Fargo threw a right forearm block to deflect the slashing blade, and drew his revolver with his left hand, corkscrewing it up and ramming it into the man's gut. He triggered, the blast muffled by meat and bone. The man's head flew back, striking the doorway, blood fountaining from bullet punctures front and back. His honed steel blade sliced past the corded muscles of Fargo's midriff, snagging his buckskin jacket slightly, then arching harmlessly to land in the dirt.

Dead on his feet, the man began crumpling. Fargo saw the flare of the sawed-off rifle and heard a terrific roar, a slug chipping the wall behind him, and ducked reflexively as he pivoted back to the first man. Too late. Running bootfalls were retreating down the alley, and he realized that the man must have panicked and started to flee the instant he'd seen his partner had failed.

Fargo stood in angry silence, staring at the darkness into which the man had disappeared. Then, turning, he knelt to examine his attacker, who was slumped as if asleep against the wall. The man had ordinary clothes and a few ordinary effects like tobacco and a pencil stub, not much money, and no identification. His looks weren't anything worth remembering, either.

Behind Frago on the main street, a pistol cracked, and then another, the reports coming faintly from the southeast. Here in the alley it was very quiet, the confrontation having been so swift that apparently it had passed unnoticed. Nobody was shouting alarms, nobody was running to see what was wrong; it was almost as if he'd never been stopped here at all.

Fargo left it that way as he strode on to the rooming house.

A standard, two-story whitewashed farmhouse, it perched high on a great multicolored rock mound overlooking the river. Inside, the front room served as a lobby, with bedrooms upstairs and owner's quarters in the rest of the downstairs. The owner's son slept on the sofa in the lobby and, like an obedient watchdog, arose when Fargo entered. Bleary-eyed, he grabbed a key from the pigeonhole rack and tossed it to Fargo. Fargo shook his head.

"I'm in Room Four. This key is stamped number twelve."

"Don't matter. Any key fits any lock."

"So that's how the mouse got in. You got a trap?"

Sleepily the son rummaged around and found a common catch-spring mousetrap. He apologized for not having bait, calling as Fargo was going up the stairs. "If you're worried about the key, put a chair against the door."

Room Four had a chair, which Fargo promptly wedged under the knob. It also had a humpbacked bed, a tall wardrobe, and a combination bureau and washstand. On the floor were his saddlebags, on the bureau was a hobnail lamp with a tasseled shade, and on the washstand was a bowl and cracked pitcher.

Fargo lit the lamp, drew the window shade, took his gun-cleaning kit from his saddlebags, and hauled his Sharps rifle out of the wardrobe. Carefully he cleaned the Sharps and loaded a fresh charge, thinking of Fat Dan as he did so. Crossing Tobin was a fairly cut-and-dried affair with about as much subtlety as a buffalo's prick.

Otis Wyndam and his train, however, now that was bamboozling. Each section made an average-sized train, big enough to provide reasonable security without being unwieldable. Yet trains can be any size; it shouldn't have mattered to Wyndam if more folks joined than he bargained for, and to travel a week apart due to petty wrangling showed rotten leadership. Still, they'd probably muddle through if winter held off and they didn't detour according to Wyndam's maps. Oh, General Isaac I. Stevens had trailblazed a government railroad survey, all right. But the path he charted in '53 ran far north from upper Montana to Fort Walla Walla on the Washington side of the Columbia River. Otis Wyndam wsa either stupid or a liar . . . and the land promoter had not looked stupid.

Propping his Sharps by the bed, Fargo decided on a quick cat bath before retiring. He peeled off his clothes and proceeded to wash away the grime. He was working with the towel when he heard someone stop out in the hall, and knuckles tapped softly on his door.

"Hello?" Are you awake?"

He recognized Velvet's voice, her whisper pleasant and innocuous enough. But Fargo had been lured before by sweet-sounding traps, and instinctively he checked that the shade and lock remained closed and undisturbed, while padding to the door and clasping the towel modestly around his waist.

"What do you want?"

"What . . . ! What d'you think I want, you lout."

Cautiously he pressed his ear against the door panel. He heard no creak of shuffling boots and no low breathing of men out in the hall with her.

Velvet said somewhat testily, "You going to let me deliver or make me keep yakking to myself?"

Fargo relented. Removing the chair from under the knob, he warily unlatched, then opened the door. Velvet slipped in. She leaned against the door, shutting it and relocking it with her hands behind her. She

had changed from her dance-hall costume into a bur-
gundy wrapper, and as she stepped toward Fargo,
smiling, her figure stretched the garment, revealing
intriguing curves and points of interest. She was not
carrying anything. In fact, she appeared not to have
come with anything, period, save her wrapper and a
pair of ankle-length serge shoes.

Fargo said guardedly. "I'm not fit for visitors. What's
the gag?"

"I gave you a kiss, you gave me a present. You also
gave me a kiss, then, so now I must give you a present. It is our custom." She moved closer, letting her
gown sweep back behind her, her eyes mocking. "I've
only one thing of value, but I'm giving it freely, yours
just for the taking."

Fargo was still suspicious. "Great. I'll unwrap it
later."

"Oh, no, it's my gift to give." With an open mouth
and slowly sliding tongue, she kissed him again, lazily,
sensuously. "I'm no society belle virgin, all coyness
and tease," she murmured. "I'm rich man's baggage,
remember? Fat Dan's honeypot, lately, and I willingly
admit it."

"Bluntly, too."

"If there's anything this country does, it strips away
the nonessentials." Laughing throatily, she shrugged
off her wrapper.

Fargo couldn't help but smile. Velvet was a sensu-
ous product, provocatively packaged. She looked up
into his face and he could see that she seemed not only
willing, but eagerly anticipating her gift-giving. She
exuded sex, a blatant desire for it, and Fargo reacted
lustily as her wrapper slid slowly to her feet, revealing
her smooth, round breasts and the crescent between
her tapering thighs. She raised her arms slightly to
hold his shoulder with one hand and loosen his grip on

the towel with the other. The towel almost hooked upon his growing erection, which she regarded delightedly.

"Oh, you're fit. Lordy, are you fit."

As she kicked off her shoes, Fargo braced the chair against the door again. He then threw his clothes off the bed and pulled her to him by the waist, lowering her onto the coverlet. He crawled in alongside her, kissing her breasts, suckling her nipples while his hands parted her sensitive loins, his fingers caressing, massaging as he eased his way inside.

Velvet sighed and mewed with growing arousal, her body undulating against him, her own hand slipping between them to rub and fondle him. "C'mon, sport," she panted, "Now, do it now . . ."

Fargo rose and knelt over her. She lay silent with anticipation, her legs spread on either side of him, her exposed pink furrow moist and throbbing. He levered downward, and she gasped with the rock-hard feel of him as he began his gentle entry. She pushed upward, her thighs clasping him, swallowing his full thick length up inside her.

"Lordy, lordy," she moaned, her muscles squeezing around him so tightly that Fargo almost cried out from the pleasure. He thrust, and she automatically responded in rhythm, mewing deep in her throat, her splayed thighs arching spasmodically against his pumping hips. Their pace increased, and increased again, their passion mounting greedily.

Soon their rhythm grew frenzied. She rolled him over, he rolled her over, back and forth, their nude bodies frantic in their pounding madness. Fargo's breath rasped in his throat; Velvet's legs cramped where they gripped his middle. There was nothing but exquisite sensation, no existence beyond the boundaries of their flesh.

Velvet squealed as her climax struck. Her nails raked Fargo's back with each spasm, her limbs jerking violently. Fargo felt his own swift orgasm, his juices spewing hotly into her. She absorbed all of his flowing passion, until, with a final convulsion, she lay still, satiated.

"Never with Fat Dan," she sighed blissfully. "Never like that." She stretched her legs back so she could lie with him inside her, and they dozed off, their bodies gently intertwined . . .

Fargo awoke once to Velvet kissing him. Again they made love, savoring each fresh touch of their naked flesh, and afterward she cuddled againt him while they sank back into lethargy, and Fargo drifted off to sleep again . . .

He awoke a second time to a sharp *kersnap*! and a sudden yelp of a feminine voice. He sat up, hearing slightly muffled whimpers as though someone was crying through a mouthful of fingers. It was still dark, but he didn't know the time and really didn't care, intrigued by the dim outline of a naked young woman prancing with lively grace, removing her hand from her mouth and waving it about while moaning and mewing and cussing like a sailor.

Fargo burst out laughing.

"What a rotten trick!" she rebuked, stopping now and dipping her hands between her legs. "You should've warned me you had that sack booby-trapped."

"Mousetrapped, Velvet. To catch small rats."

"That's not fair! I worked hard to find where you hid it."

"You sure did. What're you going to tell Fat Dan?"

"I don't know. Something." She padded to the bed and flung the trap at Fargo. "Oh, you ruined everything. This was my big chance, and once I'd got it, I was going to vamoose on Fat Dan and everyone."

Fargo gave her a soft smile. "You can dress now."

Velvet hesitated for a moment, then climbed on the bed, her face screwed up into a little girl's pout. "Why do I have to? It's not morning yet, and I bet if we try, we can get something up before the sun . . ."